Indoo Seth is a Delhi-based entrepreneur. Born to a Punjabi restaurateur family, she grew up in Kolkata. After finishing a design, marketing and retailing course at The American College in London, she ventured into garment manufacturing, and turned out to be a successful exporter. Currently, she trades in real estate.

Women's empowerment is a cause she strongly believes in. One of her endeavours is to help the underprivileged women and the girl child in the community.

Going for long walks and travelling around the world are things she loves doing.

EMOTIONAL HOSTAGE

Indoo Seth

OM
Om Books International

First published in 2015 by

OM
Om Books International

Corporate & Editorial Office
A-12, Sector 64, Noida 201 301
Uttar Pradesh, India
Phone: +91 120 477 4100
Email: editorial@ombooks.com
Website: www.ombooksinternational.com

Sales Office
107, Darya Ganj, New Delhi 110 002, India
Phone: +91 11 4000 9000, 2326 3363, 2326 5303
Fax: +91 11 2327 8091
Email: sales@ombooks.com
Website: www.ombooks.com

Disclaimer: This is a work of fiction. Any resemblance to actual incidents, events or persons (living or dead) is purely coincidental. These are personal views of the author and do not intend to hurt the feelings and sentiments of any individual or a community.

ISBN: 978-93-83202-28-7

Printed in India

10 9 8 7 6 5 4 3 2 1

For

My parents, who have allowed me to live life on my own terms
and for being my strongest pillars of support.
Thank you both. I miss you dearly.

My friend, Gazala Kehan, who left us in 2010.
The vacuum of your friendship is yet to be filled.

Loneliness can, at times, spiral into desperation, pushing one onto paths that, under ordinary circumstances, one may never have tread.

– Anonymous

CHAPTER 1

'I don't play cards. I am sure it will be quite a boring affair,' Simran said firmly. Her two best friends looked at her beseechingly.

Diwali was just a fortnight away and one was just starting to feel the nip in the air. The social circuit of Delhi was busy hosting card parties. Madhu and Ruby had been invited to a big card party and were trying to persuade Simran to accompany them. She was in no mood to hobnob with strangers and that too at a gathering where she would be sticking out like a sore thumb, for playing cards was one habit she had never wanted to acquire.

So, for the past half hour she had been trying her best to field off their persuasive skills; citing illness, work or some other commitment, but it was all in vain.

In her mid-30s, Simran was slim and attractive, but it was her confident demeanour that invited a second look from many. Simran was going through an emotionally turbulent phase, and gradually coming to terms with her single status again. She kept herself busy trading in the stock market and dabbling in property. Buying and selling was something she enjoyed doing once in a while. She didn't feel equipped to take up a full-time job which would require commitment, that had to wait till she was feeling emotionally settled again. She was strong-minded and confident and knew this was just a passing phase and she would bounce back sooner than later.

Madhu married when she had just turned 20. She was content and happy being a perfect homemaker. Life never steered beyond her husband Raghav and two daughters; she wanted to give her best to them. She was quiet, affable, and though naïve, was more level-headed among the three friends; always the one mitigating arguments and calling for peace. As opposed to her two best friends, she was on the heavier side, with shoulder-length hair framing her pretty round face blessed with flawless skin. It was only in the company of her two friends that she ventured to do anything out of the ordinary.

Of the three friends, Ruby was the head-turner; five feet seven inches tall, with long, straight hair cascading down her back. She was outspoken to a fault, a fashionista who had a zest for everything she did. She was in a happy space with the man in her life, Anil. She lived with her parents and was years younger than her two buddies. Ruby was the practical one and rarely accepted things at face value. Her profession as a fashion consultant, where she met different types of people, gave her the experience and confidence to judge people faster. Madhu and Simran often adhered to the diktats of their hearts over their heads and were often castigated by Ruby for not being pragmatic. Trusting all and sundry was not Ruby's forte.

The three spent many of their evenings together—shopping, dining or simply spending time at each other's homes—chatting and catching up on each other's lives. Each of them had their own individuality; but their sweet and silly little quirks and the fact that they were romantics at heart made them companions.

'You will have loads of fun. What's the point in being on your own? You will only be fretting over unnecessary things. At least come with us so that we can all be together,' Ruby interjected, trying to persuade Simran.

Simran smiled. She appreciated the love and concern of her friends. After her divorce, Ruby and Madhu had become more protective; watching over her like mother hens. They ensured that she was never left alone and were always around when all she probably needed was just a hug. They knew she was vulnerable and alone with no family in Delhi, and wanted her to ride the low phase with a strong support system. Simran loved having them around; for her, they were family. The trio had been the best of friends for years but were going through different phases in their lives.

After the divorce, Simran had decided to send her nine-year-old daughter Karishma, to her parents' place in Chennai. She felt her parents would give her daughter a more stable environment, as she was attempting to start life afresh. She bore no animosity towards her ex-husband; the divorce had been mutual on the grounds of irreconcilable differences. Though the overwhelming emotion was that of relief and freedom, she, at times did ponder over uncertainties. She often wondered when she would be able to bring Karishma back to live with her. It was not an easy decision to send her child away but the family mutually decided that would be the best for the child's emotional well-being in the long run. Living alone was also not something Simran was used to. She knew she had made this decision against all odds and had forced her parents to accept her choice to stay in Delhi. Most of her friends were friendly with her ex-husband, she didn't want to be part of a group where she was being told details about his life or vice versa. Living in the same city, with an ex-husband in it, wasn't comforting either; she just didn't want their paths to cross.

The feeling of picking herself up and starting life again from scratch made her jittery sometimes; who would she turn to for guidance? The emotional trauma after a divorce was also daunting. The pause phase and healing were necessary for her to get her thoughts in order, besides the thought of not having her daughter enjoy the support of a father—something that most kids took for granted—was distressing. However, she strongly felt that she could not have given Karishma a happy environment at home if she had continued to live with her now ex-husband. Karishma was mature for her age and would not be happy till her mother was happy. It had been a tough decision, but in her view, a good and a necessary one.

Living all by herself was an entirely new experience for Simran. Festivals especially were a family affair and even with her friends, who were busy with their respective Diwali preparations, she often felt like a bystander. Her family had wanted her to celebrate the festival in Chennai, but she wanted some time on her own to put her life into perspective. She however did admit to herself that the festival days would be lonely.

She did not want to go for this card party because she was in no mood to live through the expectations of the happening parties of Delhi society; the fierce competition to look one's best, exchange the most expensive gifts, gossip about things bordering on the inane and then the pressure of being demoted to list B and C. Anyway, they were just arbitrary grades signifying social status.

Simran believed that she lacked the most important criterion for entry into the hallowed circle, money. But that was not important. She wanted to focus on larger things. The need to get her career on track was of utmost importance. She desired to have her own export factory and invest her earnings into real estate. She wanted to earn enough to bring Karishma back to Delhi. She believed in her baby steps and knew that only strict focus would bring her life on track again.

'It will be nice to meet new people, Simran. You know I would not be going there myself if it was one of those over the top affairs,' Madhu added.

Simran knew that she had lost the bout. 'Ok, this one is for you, Madhu. You owe me big time for this, because I know what kind of a torturous evening it will turn out to be.'

CHAPTER 2

That evening they drove into the premises of Mrs Kohli's sprawling three-storied bungalow, with a tennis court along the driveway.

As the three walked in, Simran noticed that the interior was in need of a touch of paint and more; contrary to the impressive grandeur it projected on the outside. The sitting area was teeming with people gathered in smaller groups. Simran noted that most of the guests were above 50. She sighed, visualising just how the evening would turn out to be.

'What's wrong with both of you; how can you put me through this? Everyone in this room looks over 50!'

'Relax, you have just walked in, wait and watch, you will enjoy yourself,' Ruby was quick to retort.

'Yes sure,' she rolled her eyes, sarcastically, 'I would have been better off at home, watching a movie.'

It was not long before that Simran was convinced she had indeed made the wrong decision. Her friends got busy with their card games and she had to essentially take on the role of the nothing-better-to-do onlooker. However, time and again, she noticed each of her friends look around the room.

'Are you guys looking for someone?' Simran asked finally.

'Mrs Kohli's son,' Madhu responded, and added with a smile, 'He doesn't play cards either. You will enjoy his company.'

She learnt from them how they had made his acquaintance during another card party. He had been a real charmer; affable, and had easily got into a conversation with each of them. His mother was fond of hosting these pre-Diwali bashes. He did not play cards but was not averse to meeting new people.

'I haven't come with you to spend the evening with Mrs Kohli's son,' Simran interrupted her friends as they gushed about Rahul Kohli. 'If this is your idea of fun, I'm better off hibernating.'

She grumbled under her breath and wondered how had she got saddled into an evening like this?

It was well after 9:30 pm that Mrs Kohli's son finally appeared. Ruby pointed him out as he mingled with the other guests. Simran observed him as he walked around greeting people; pleasant looking with glasses which made him appear rather distinguished, he had salt and pepper hair and beard. She wondered why he sported a beard—he would have looked much younger without one. There was an air of confidence about him which was very striking. He wore a striped shirt with a blazer and held onto a can of beer.

His bean pole slimness immediately reminded her of her own weight issues. She starved herself, trying to keep her weight down after her daughter's birth. In all fairness, she liked the slim-bordering-on-thin look over a pot belly. While his upbringing was in a conventional *makke di roti-sarso da saag* type of Punjabi family, his polished demeanour was that of a private missionary school bred, evident from the intonation of the voice she overheard.

'Meet my good friend, Simran,' said Madhu, when they finally came face to face, 'And Simran, this is Rahul.'

He extended his hand. It was a firm handshake.

'Hi! Nice to meet you,' he responded and looked Simran straight in the eye. He then turned to look at Madhu and Ruby, 'Are you girls enjoying? Sorry, just got back from work.'

'Oh yes. We just got here a short while ago. Do you always work so late?' Ruby asked.

'I usually get back around nine. Once the office shuts, I catch up on a lot of pending stuff. Aren't you all going to play cards?'

'We just finished a game. Actually, Simran doesn't play cards, so we took a break, just to give her company.'

'I don't play either! So that makes the two of us,' Rahul responded, once again looking at Simran straight in the eye, and smiled.

Simran felt an odd sensation in her stomach; for a fraction of a second, as he looked at her, he seemed to have swept her away from her companions into a strange camaraderie of their own. She was impressed by his way with words.

'So, can we depend on you to ensure that she doesn't get bored?' Madhu asked, breaking the moment.

'Absolutely! Just give me a few minutes. I will greet some of the other guests and head right back,' Rahul confirmed.

Simran just smiled. But she was fuming inside; angry that her friends had decided to conveniently palm her off to some stranger just so that they could get busy with their card games.

'Oh, that's great! Thank you Rahul, that's so sweet of you,' Madhu added, and Simran saw Ruby mirroring the same appreciation.

'Please don't dump me on his head! It's his party and he has to play host,' Simran said angrily when Rahul had moved on. 'You girls go ahead and play. There is no need to trouble somebody else, just because you don't want to feel guilty about dragging me to this boring party.'

'How can we leave you alone? Let's see if we can find another familiar face to introduce you to,' Madhu looked around anxiously.

'Don't worry, I will hang around for a while and then come and sit with one of you.'

Simran could not even leave, having offered to be their chauffer for the evening. Well, she told herself, she could do this for her friends who were always around when she needed them.

As Madhu and Ruby moved towards the card tables again Simran got her attention focused on the gathering. It could be an amusing pastime, she told herself, as she noted the atypical clothes and mannerisms of the people; the swelling nouveau riche was busy talking about their millions and their balance sheets. She didn't have either, to be particularly proud of, but stood nodding and smiled politely at what she thought were absolutely vacuous topics of conversation.

But amusement soon gave way to boredom. She almost started wishing she would find somebody to drive her friends home. She could then escape unnoticed! It is when she was almost desperately looking around that Rahul waylaid her.

'Hey Simran, there you are. I have been looking for you. I thought you managed to hoodwink your friends and run away,' he said in good humour, and added, 'I can completely identify with your desire to yawn at the faces of these people.'

Simran smiled at his perception. Was she really this transparent, she wondered!

There was an awkward silence between the two as both started looking around; they had nothing to say to each other and therefore, were compelled to overhear the conversations in the vicinity.

'I've just got back from Shimla, Ramesh. What a beautiful hill station. I have been there so many times, but in autumn it is absolutely enchanting,' said the gentleman who had earlier introduced himself to Simran as Mr Batra.

'Why were you there at this time of the year? Wasn't it really cold?' Ramesh asked.

'No, it was fantastic. I've just bought a house on an acre of land with a superb view and I had to sign all the papers and pay the balance before taking possession.'

'Must have been expensive, if it is on an acre,' Ramesh obviously could not help asking.

'No, not very, I got it at a bargain, for two crores. The seller wanted to offload the property in winter and didn't have the patience to wait till summer,' Mr Batra responded, proving what an astute investor he was and that for him two crores were like pennies.

'Ramesh, you must come to Shimla in summer with your family,' he told his friend.

'Thanks! But I want to buy something in London this summer, so I plan to take the family there.'

Of course, Ramesh had to triumph over the measly two crores! Not one to give up easily, Mr Batra replied, 'London is not a good idea. Return on investment is very low and also capital appreciation is currently very slow.'

'I'm just buying a house to enjoy the summer with my family. I will just keep it locked when I'm not there. Kids are also growing up and they may want to study in the UK,' Ramesh said offhandedly.

Simran by now was desperately trying not to laugh out loud. She suddenly became aware that Rahul was staring at her.

'Don't you play cards?' she asked, attempting to make small talk, although she already knew the answer to that. She was feeling guilty that Ruby and Madhu had literally arm-twisted him to give her company.

'No, it's a vice I don't indulge in; no minor vices for me,' he said, looking at her intently, almost willing her to ask him more.

There was something in the way he was looking at her! And she could not keep herself from responding, 'Really, so what are the vices you indulge in?'

'Now that's telling, let's save that for another time,' he replied ambiguously. To change the topic, he asked, 'I have not seen you around. Are you from Delhi?'

'I am from Chennai, but I live in Delhi now,' Simran replied.

'Delhi can be a brutal city if you are on your own.'

'I think I have been lucky; haven't had too much of a problem. This city treats me well.'

'I am sure it does–it treats all attractive women well. So do you stay in Delhi with your husband?'

'No, I am divorced.'

To her relief he did not probe further. She definitely would not have been comfortable discussing her personal life with a perfect stranger.

'Don't you play cards?' he asked. Simran felt like an idiot! He must be wondering what she was doing at a card party if she didn't play cards.

'No, I really don't have the patience,' Simran said awkwardly. 'Please move on to your other guests. I will join Madhu and Ruby,' she added.

'I'm not the host. It's my mother's party. Come let me get you a drink. You don't mind walking to the bar I hope. I wouldn't like to miss the opportunity of escorting a good-looking lady,' he said.

He was flirting with her, Simran realised, but unlike the offending ways that other men used.

Over the years, she had always been quick to brush aside any unwarranted overture. She was especially wary of male attention now after her divorce. Being labelled as *easy game* was something she definitely was averse to. But far from being offended at Rahul's remark, she admitted, his attempts to get friendly were actually amusing. *Am I attracted to him,* she asked herself.

Just then, a lady walked across the room to where they were talking. Rahul was obviously surprised to see her as was evident from his expression. The lady stood silent for some time, shifting her gaze from Rahul to Simran and back.

Did Rahul know her? Simran wondered. For a couple of minutes the three of them looked at each other till Rahul seemed to make up his mind and move forward.

'Simran, this is my wife Sonia.'

'Hi.' Sonia's curt greeting, accompanied by a plastic smile, was directed to no one in particular.

Simran was startled to see Rahul's better half. Madhu and Ruby had not mentioned that he was married. And why was Rahul not comfortable in her presence? Sonia too did not make an effort to start a conversation. It was possible that she did not do so in the presence of strangers. As she turned to look around the room full of guests, Simran looked at her.

A good-looking woman, she must have been really attractive in her younger days, Simran thought. However, there was a cold, unaffected air about her; as though she could not be bothered with what was happening around her. Dressed to the hilt, like the other women in the room, she looked around with a blank expression on her face. Simran had never met a couple who was so dissimilar; Sonia stood there, absolutely quiet, talking to no one, while Rahul seemed to have something to say to everybody he ran into.

Simran herself was reserved with strangers, avoiding crowds and the usual brouhaha of social occasions, but even she couldn't muster up a few words for such moments.

The only thing she picked up from Sonia was an icy hostility. *I guess she does not like me*, Simran wondered... *Maybe Sonia did not like anyone unfamiliar*, she concluded.

They stood awkwardly for minutes, which only seemed to drag on. Sonia then suddenly moved away to talk to other guests. Simran was trying to figure out what to make of this strange encounter when Rahul asked her suddenly, 'Simran, are you interested in art?'

Why was he quiet, when his wife was with us, Simran couldn't help wondering. 'Well, I'm not a collector, but if there is something worth seeing, I would be able to appreciate it,' was her quick reply.

'Great, I have a small collection, would you like to have a look?' he asked.

'What kind of art?' Simran was surprised at this offer. He had just met her for the first time today.

'Some frames I bought in Germany. It is on the first floor. Come, I'll show you; I'm sure you will like it.'

Simran hesitated. *Would it be ok to leave the party with him and go to the private quarters of the family?*

Judging from Sonia's recent behaviour, Simran was unsure if the wife would interpret it otherwise. She felt that Delhi wives tended to keep an eye on their husbands at such parties, looking out for real and imaginary liaisons. Simran definitely did not want to give Sonia a reason to come charging to stake a claim on her possession. She anyway disliked the mindset that single women were out to entrap the gullible married men. *But what the hell,* she told herself, *it would be better than standing and staring at each other's faces.* Rahul obviously felt obligated to be by her side. Once again, she mentally cursed her friends for sweet talking him into giving her company. For a second, she wondered *how Rahul's wife would react to this invitation.* Then she chided herself for these thoughts. She was going to see the paintings; not on a romantic tryst, for heaven's sake!

Simran climbed the stairs with Rahul; no one paid any heed, they were all engrossed in their respective card games.

'Who are your favourite artists?' Rahul asked her.

'Frankly, I don't have much of a clue. I am just an admirer,' she said bluntly.

'Well, art should grow on a person, I bought one from a famous artist two years ago and now I hate looking at it—it puts me into depression.'

Simran could not help laughing.

'Why don't you sell it?' she asked finally.

'No one seems to like it, can't get it off my back, don't know what I was thinking when I bought it.'

They had reached the landing by then and Rahul stood facing her.

'Put it up in your guest washroom. It will be out of sight,' Simran suggested.

'What a great idea! You are a genius.'

They started laughing, almost simultaneously. Simran had often been complimented on how her eyes lit up when she laughed. Rahul stopped abruptly. But his eyes never left her face. He stood there just looking at her; without uttering a word. Simran too stopped laughing; feeling a strange frisson of excitement in her heart. The intensity of his gaze made her want to look away, but she could not. And then suddenly he smiled and the moment passed.

What just happened back there? Simran asked herself, as Rahul led her back to the party. She hadn't even focused on the painting!

As the evening wore on, Simran realised that Rahul could be a real charmer. She enjoyed all the attention, flirted with him and even chose to ignore when his arm lingered on a few seconds longer at her waist as he directed her to where Ruby and Madhu stood; perhaps with the knowledge that it would all end the minute she stepped out of his gate. She was surprised at her own confusion; she liked him, but then, she disliked flirts. She dismissed her thoughts knowing they were plain rubbish and just a fabrication of her boredom.

'Have you seen his wife? I heard rumours that he does not get along with her. Surprising, considering he is such a hit with the other women you see around,' Ruby voiced her confusion when Rahul had moved on to some other guests.

'Quite a ladies' man if you ask me! Why did he take you for a stroll around his house?' Madhu asked, suddenly sounding wary.

'I had gone with him to see his painting collection,' Simran interrupted, crossing her fingers that they would not ask her about it. 'Why is he suddenly the villain of the piece, guys? You practically dropped me on his head a short while ago.'

'Well, he sure has taken to you Simran. I can see that in his eyes and body language,' Ruby said perceptively.

Before Simran could respond to that, Rahul joined them again to say that dinner had been served.

For the rest of the evening, Rahul was a good host. Simran enjoyed his company and was particularly taken in by the fact that he was not excessively inquisitive about her personal life.

When it was finally time to leave, Madhu and Ruby went off to thank Mrs Kohli for the evening.

Simran was standing by the door, waiting, when Rahul walked up to her, 'We must connect again; it was really nice meeting you,' he said, affably.

'Sure, sounds great.'

'Can I call you? We could meet for coffee sometime.'

She rattled her number and noticed that he didn't save it on his phone or write it down. *He will surely not remember it later*, she told herself. But then wondered *why Rahul, a married man, would single her out to ask for her number.* But, she dismissed the thought.

'If only he was single, this evening would not have been a wasted one for Simran.' These were Ruby's first words when they were alone in the car.

'Single? Who...who are you talking about?' asked a perplexed Madhu.

Simran however understood the drift of Ruby's words and who she was talking about.

'Are you sure you are not interested in him yourself. You would make quite a striking couple,' Simran tried to catch Ruby's expression in the rear-view mirror.

'And leave Anil? Not for all the Rahuls in the world.'

Madhu finally caught on. 'Why can't you both look for simple, single eligible men that you would really want to settle down with?'

'Oh no! Not again,' Ruby and Simran shouted in unison. They were always dodging Madhu's attempts to play the matchmaker. Madhu joined in the laughter that followed.

By the time Simran dropped her friends home and reached her own place she was exhausted. Rahul had faded from her thoughts by the time she fell asleep.

~

Rahul, in the meanwhile, went to bed distracted; he couldn't eliminate Simran from his thoughts. It had been a while since he was attracted to any woman, and he found it impossible to get Simran out of his mind. Sonia, his wife, lay next to him; it had been years since she aroused any amorous feelings in him. He remembered his first meeting with her, as arranged by his parents. She was just the woman he wanted to marry; she was a good wife and the perfect daughter-in-law, but why was he so disenchanted by her now? He remembered the times when they would sit together in the garden, in the morning, catching up with each other over cups of tea, or just reading the newspaper. But now, he was always racing against time to reach office and she was busy with the children. When did the romance leave their marriage?

Simran's smile, her way with words, her sense of humour, her dressing style kept creeping into Rahul's thoughts. He made a resolve to call her, the first thing in the morning. He could still smell her perfume and the desire to hold her in his arms was overwhelming. He debated with himself and concluded that he had the right to love again.

CHAPTER 3

Simran woke up to an indolent day. It was almost noon and she cursed herself for sleeping in so late. She should have been in front of the television at least an hour ago monitoring how the stock market was faring. Now she would have to call her broker for all the news and hope that she had made some profits. She reached for the phone to call him and realised that the man had been trying to get through to her number and left at least eight missed calls. Drat! She remembered putting it on the silent mode after she got back home late last night.

But on a closer scrutiny, she found it was not the broker's number in the missed call list. Whose number was this? Who could have called so early in the day? Probably one of those pesky annoying callers trying to sell insurance or credit card!

There was a new message in her inbox:

Hi, this is Rahul. I guess you are either sleeping in or you get to work really early. What do you do anyway? We never got around to discussing that yesterday... Will call back.

The events of the previous evening ran through Simran's mind. She had actually enjoyed the attention.

Simran went and stood in front of the long mirror in her bedroom. *Did he fancy her...*she asked herself? Why would he call her otherwise? And he actually remembered her number. She felt flattered and elated by this innocuous phone call. After all, he was a good looking man!

Simran lived in her own apartment. She felt secure with a roof over her head. Her father, a businessman, had been generous and bought her a two-bedroom flat in south Delhi and a car to make life easier for his only daughter. He was affluent and had his own trading company which dealt with commodities. He didn't want his daughter struggling to maintain a decent lifestyle. Simran had put all her savings in a fixed deposit and had enough to run her expenses. But if she ever ran short of funds her father always came to her rescue. She knew it wouldn't be long before she would take up a job in an export house to learn the tricks of the trade.

As she went about her chores, Rahul continued to wriggle into her thoughts repeatedly. She remembered how last night she had brushed aside Ruby's insinuations. Then why did the fact that he had called the very next day uplift her spirits? *Would he really call back*, she wondered. She had had her share of crushes, but this was definitely something exceptional. She felt a flutter in her heart as she thought of Rahul and reminded herself that she was not a gawky teenager anymore. And added to that, Simran was foolishly nurturing thoughts about a man who belonged to someone else.

Time seemed to crawl by as she waited. She thought about the party and how Rahul had been attentive to her throughout the evening; leaving her side only for brief intervals. There was something different about him from the other men she usually came across. He was courteous and did not try to get overfriendly, even after a couple of drinks.

This time when the phone rang she almost ran to pick it up.

'Hi, what's up? Did I wake you up?' Ruby asked.

'Woke up a short while ago, but feeling very tired; these late nights don't suit me,' Simran responded, trying not to sound disappointed–that it was not Rahul–from her voice.

'Sleep later in the afternoon... What's your plan today, want to see a movie?' Ruby asked, in her usual effervescent way.

'Don't you guys have to go for another card party tonight? What about Anil? Don't you have any plans with him?'

'Of course I do! The card party is only after dinner, around 10, and Anil will be coming along too. Let's see a six o'clock show.'

'Sounds like a plan! You decide which one and I will pick you up at five thirty in the evening...but please, Bollywood.'

'Ok done. Did you have a good time yesterday?'

'It was nice. Mrs Kohli is a gracious hostess. How are you guys friendly with her, she is much older?' Simran asked.

'Actually we met her during the card season last year. We have a common friend who took us to her house. She is known in the city for her parties; her card parties in particular are very popular. You know how Madhu and I love playing cards.'

'And I was your lucky charm. I noticed you both beaming after winning several games,' Simran laughed and added.

'Oh! You noticed us? I thought you had eyes only for Rahul,' Ruby immediately retorted.

'Don't be silly Ruby. I was just being polite to your acquaintance. He too was just being a gracious host,' Simran tried to brush off Ruby's observation.

'Who are you kidding, Simran? It was evident every time he looked at you,' Ruby pointed out. She added with a laugh, 'Sweetie, we have been to his house over a dozen times, he has never offered to show us his paintings.'

'Maybe I look an arty type,' Simran suggested.

'Sure and we look the card-playing type!'

Simran laughed out aloud.

Ruby went quiet suddenly.

'What are you thinking about? Are you jealous that your old friend is giving more attention to his new acquaintance?' Simran joked.

Ruby sounded serious.

'Jokes aside Simran, please remember that Rahul is a married man. He can be charming and it would be easy to fall for him. Even though we know that he is *unhappily married*, his marital status cannot be overlooked.'

Simran was surprised at the sudden change in Ruby's tone. 'Chill! I am not interested in getting involved with anybody right now,' Simran attempted to assure her friend.

But she knew she did not sound convincing, even to herself. She was hoping that Ruby would disconnect soon as she was expecting Rahul to call back.

Before the friends ended the call, Ruby asked Simran to call her up immediately if she received a call from Rahul. Ruby was sure to make a mountain out of a molehill and Simran did not need anybody breathing down her neck with unwarranted advice. Simran had barely put the phone down when it rang again. It was Rahul.

'Lady, you can really go on and on! Your number has been busy for the last 20 minutes.'

'Who is this?' she feigned ignorance.

'Well, if you can forget my voice in a few hours there isn't much to say. Maybe I didn't create the kind of impression I thought I did last night. And you didn't save my number after I sent you a text. You've broken my heart!' Rahul said, with a chuckle.

She smiled, enjoying the fact that he was now openly flirting with her. 'Oh! Did we meet last night? Please forgive me, but I met quite a few people, so who would this be?'

'I thought I had kept you to myself last evening, Simran. It seems I didn't do a good job,' he responded, sounding disappointed.

Simran started laughing. 'I didn't know all that attention was to deliberately keep me away from the others.'

'Aha! So you do know who I am.'

'Yes Rahul, what a pleasant surprise!' she said.

'It was wonderful spending time with you last evening. My mother loves playing cards and she keeps inviting her friends. I am glad you guys came over; I didn't know she had such young interesting friends.'

'Honestly speaking, I don't know your mother. Madhu and Ruby just dragged me along,' Simran admitted.

'Well, my good luck then; so glad you came over. Hope you are going to join them again when they come over the next time,' Rahul asked.

'But I don't play cards... So I don't think...'

There was a moment's silence. It was as though the two of them did not know how to take the conversation forward.

'When are you inviting me over for a cup of coffee?' Rahul said abruptly.

Simran was not expecting this and didn't know how to field the question immediately.

'It would be a pleasure. Whenever,' Simran responded after a moment's hesitation.

'Give me a date and time and I will be there.'

'Come over for coffee tomorrow, around five, if you are free,' Simran suggested.

'Sure, I will be there.'

Later, Simran asked herself *why she let him practically invite himself over. Yes, I liked his company, but he was being more than just friendly!*

To hell with unnecessary caution, Simran finally told herself. She would just go with the flow. What could be inappropriate about having a cup of coffee with a friend? *Friend... When did he become one?* she asked herself.

The next day Simran was anxious, waiting for the clock to strike five in the evening. She went through her wardrobe a zillion times, wishing to look her best. At last it was five and the doorbell rang promptly. She was impressed.

Rahul walked into her home, with a box of expensive chocolates which he placed on the table, pecked her cheek and made himself comfortable on the sofa in the sitting room–as though he had been to her house innumerable times before.

Simran knew why he had piqued her interest. He was a confident man; comfortable in his own skin, which was so not her.

'Do you live here on your own?' was his opening question, when he had settled down with his coffee.

'Yes.'

'What about your family. Are they in Delhi?'

'No, my parents live in Chennai. So does my daughter.'

'You have a daughter? How old is she? Do you like living on your own?'

'She is old enough to understand that her mother needs time to sort out her life,' she responded and was amazed at how easy it was for her to share this detail of her personal life with him. 'Yes, I like my independence. I have a group of single and married friends who treat me like their extended family. So, I don't miss not having my family around; I know I have a shoulder if need be.' Simran replied proudly.

'That is disappointing,' Rahul said.

Simran's face showed her surprise.

Rahul continued with a smile, 'After our conversation last night when you told me that you were single, I had been hoping to be the shoulder you could lean on.'

Simran burst out laughing and this broke the ice for the rest of the evening.

It seemed like they had been friends for years. Rahul spoke about his travels and his business. Simran soon realised that Rahul could charm anybody with his words. He was well-read, well-travelled and embraced life with open arms, something that she found quite charming. People usually were too daunted by what others might think as right or wrong.

He was neither too inquisitive about her personal life nor did he talk about his family. She decided that she was not going to probe either. Several times during the evening she checked herself from listening, almost staring, at him with rapt attention.

Two hours went by like two minutes and she felt a tug in her heart when he finally got up to leave. When he hugged her and said goodbye, the embrace did seem lengthier than usual, but, she acknowledged it was not the lecherous kind.

She had barely walked back into her bedroom when the phone rang. It was Rahul.

'Thanks so much, I really had a great time. Let's have coffee the same time tomorrow? I have a meeting in your area.'

She was amused at how easily he had taken it for granted that she would be ok to meet him the next day. *But who was I trying to fool?* she asked herself. She was attracted to him and would not hesitate to cancel her other commitments the following evening to spend time with him. She was perhaps being ludicrous, but she was willing to let her heart rule this time. So she promptly went about rescheduling her appointments.

Rahul was punctual the next evening too; a habit she respected. Conversation flowed easily and once again she was overwhelmed by Rahul's charm and sense of humour.

'I'm off to Chennai day after tomorrow to visit my daughter; I will be gone for two weeks,' Simran said.

'Do you go often?'

'Every six weeks–it's a promise I made to myself when I decided to leave Karishma with my parents. I get very restless otherwise and worry about them.'

'I'm just getting to know you, why don't you go later?'

'No Rahul. It will be difficult to change my plans; I don't like to break my promise to Karishma, but will be back in 10 days.' Simran noticed the disappointment on his face.

'Call me when you get back,' Rahul said when he left.

Will he call me when I am in Chennai, Simran asked herself. *But then, why should he? We just happen to know each other and enjoy chatting over coffee. I know that he likes me, nothing more. Do I want it to be something more?*

She had a good trip and decided to extend it for another week. There was nothing so urgent for her to return to, or was there? Rahul did cross her mind several times but she was not going to call him. She would rather wait for his call. Even if either one of the three friends was travelling, they made sure to stay in touch. During one of her usual calls Madhu casually said, 'By the way, we went to Mrs Kohli's house yesterday to play cards and Rahul asked about you. I was surprised he remembered. I told him you were away in Chennai. He wanted to know when you would be back. I wasn't sure so I didn't say anything.'

Simran soon returned to Delhi and got back into her routine. Rahul did not feature in her thoughts.

~

Some months later, as she was walking around South Extension market, she felt somebody tap her on her shoulder. It was Rahul. They spontaneously gave each other a hug. She was surprised and even more so at how happy she was to see him, even after months. He was his usual effervescent self.

'Aye stranger, how have you been?'

'All well,' she smiled. 'What are you doing here?'

He ignored the question.

'When did you get back, have you been in Chennai all these months?' he asked.

'No, no,' she laughed. 'I had gone for a few weeks only. How have you been?'

'No call lady... You have forgotten me so easily.' Rahul laughed, as he said this.

Simran laughed too. 'I was just busy doing things.'

'Let's have coffee if you are free. I'm sure there must be some nice place in the market.'

'Another time; have to go for a book launch at seven.'

'Hope you are not trying to avoid me,' he said, with his eyes intent. He then smiled and added, 'How about tomorrow...if you are free, of course.'

Simran was caught unawares, but recovered quickly, 'Sounds like a plan.'

'Fantastic. Your place tomorrow, at seven in the evening.'

Simran was amused but delighted. Something about this man made her feel good. She didn't mind him coming over.

Rahul was punctual and came at sharp seven the following evening.

The next few weeks set the pattern for their friendship. Rahul became a regular visitor to Simran's place; dropping by every other evening. How they drifted into this *every other day* pattern was baffling, but they both cherished it.

The phone calls became more frequent as did the amount of time spent together. Simran often thought about him. Each visit and each phone call added a new dimension to their friendship. And it wasn't long before that each of them acknowledged the importance of the other in their lives.

As for Simran, there was no doubt now that her heart had taken over her mind. She knew that any hope of a future with Rahul was a far-fetched one. She reminded herself several times that she was playing with fire, but she could do nothing to stop it. So she surrendered herself to her destiny. There was something that drew her to this man.

She, who had been determined to steer clear of any romantic liaison, now, had begun to count the hours she spent away from him or not talking to him. Yes, there were times when she seriously thought about Rahul's marital status. But then she had heard her friends' insinuations that all was not well between the couple. She had told herself that if a marriage did not bring one any happiness, then it anyway had no value. Hadn't she walked out of a marriage that had made her very unhappy? She could now sense a commitment from Rahul, although he had not openly stated his feelings.

This change in her life did not go unnoticed by her friends, especially Madhu and Ruby. They noted the way she now made fewer plans with them or had stopped her casual visits to their respective homes. Earlier Simran would drop by whenever she felt lonely. But now the reason to stay away was always that she needed to spend time on her own; finding her own peace of mind, watch news on television, talking to her mother or Karishma in Chennai or going through the newspaper looking to find a job in a garment factory or a buying house. She was ready to take up a full-time job and learn the tricks of the trade, which would come in handy once she started her own business. Ruby was a woman with an independent mind; she could understand Simran's need for her own space and hence took on the responsibility of assuring Madhu every time that Simran was not available.

In the meanwhile, Rahul had conquered his guilt and made up his mind to pursue Simran. Emotionally estranged from his wife, this was not the first time he had found another woman attractive. But he had never found himself so involved with the other person's company and thoughts. *What was so different here?* he had asked himself repeatedly. *Was he in love?* He knew he was treading a dangerous path. Physical attraction was something he could easily handle but his emotional reactions to Simran now came as a surprise to him; they were beyond his control. He wondered if Simran also felt the same way. He was confident that he could see a spark in Simran's eyes whenever they spent time together. He knew that she welcomed his overtures. He finally told himself that he would willingly let go of the guilt of cheating on Sonia.

CHAPTER 4

Life suddenly had taken on a new colour for Simran. She felt happy and looked forward to every date. She called their meeting time as her *happy hour*; something she cherished, and she would wait to chat with him and laugh wholeheartedly. After he left she waited for bedtime when Rahul would call again. They would talk for hours then. For Simran, these moments were very precious. Rahul's secret chat room was his study on the terrace, where he did not have to worry about being overheard. He used this room as his office at home and Sonia rarely came up to the terrace. Simran was amused at how brazen he was about calling without any hesitation; Sonia could easily get suspicious.

She often wondered about Sonia; how would she react if she ever found out about their evening meetings.

'No woman can be so blind Rahul that she does not realise that her husband has a special lady friend,' Simran observed one evening while they were sipping coffee.

'Sonia and I are together for the sake of our children. Sonia knows that. She has her own life and I have mine.

Besides, she is close to all our friends and relatives. So she spends most of her time either with them or the children.'

'But how do you stay together then? Isn't love and companionship a large part of a marriage?' Simran was curious; she also needed to understand where she stood with him. She often asked herself if she was comfortable being the *other woman* in Rahul's life.

Other woman! Ouch! It doesn't sound too well. Weren't we just close friends? Simran thought. Of course, the proximity of the 'closeness' was what Simran had to define for herself.

Rahul smiled and responded, 'Ours was an arranged marriage. Sometimes people just outgrow each other. We haven't grown together as a couple–our interests are poles apart. Our only conversations revolve around the children. Besides, there was never much love between us,' he paused, as though deep in thought, and then said, 'Love is something very special. Becoming fond of or even liking somebody is easy but love is about taking the relationship to another level. It may happen just once in a lifetime.'

Was I the love that he has never experienced?, Simran asked herself. She wanted to question further but it didn't seem like an appropriate time. *Why are you having such reckless thoughts?*, she asked herself, but just brushed it aside.

Talking about Rahul's wife was awkward, so she decided to change the topic.

She acknowledged that there was something really special between Rahul and her; more so as they had no expectations from each other. She was definitely not looking at a second marriage. Things would get too complicated. How would she explain things to her daughter? He too would not want to upset the status quo at home. She was happy with this arrangement; *it is the stolen moments that make our relationship more special*, she thought.

~

It was time to go visit her family again in Chennai. She would miss him for sure. 'Rahul, I will be visiting my parents and daughter in Chennai for three weeks.'

'Three weeks? That's a long time. How can you deprive me of such good company and for so long?' he replied, smiling.

She smiled back, 'I told you I visit my daughter and parents every six weeks. It is something I have been doing since I moved her to Chennai; I get restless otherwise. I'm missing Karishma a lot. I also want to take up a full-time job soon.'

'I understand. What kind of job?' he said, and looked at her intently.

'In a garment factory. I want to start my own business soon.'

'Sounds good.'

His face brightened as if an idea had struck him suddenly.

'I am going to Hong Kong for some days. Why don't you join me? You can carry on to Chennai then, while I return to Delhi. Please say yes... It would be nice to get away from Delhi for a while.'

She was dumbstruck! For the next few seconds, thoughts ran riot in her head. *Would it be ok to say yes? Would it be ok to go away with Rahul on a trip, that too, abroad? Would this be a clandestine rendezvous? How would my friends react to this? Should I even tell them? What about Rahul's family? And Sonia?*

Stop! The word echoed in her head... She acknowledged to herself that all these were nothing but useless doubts and in some way were making her trivialise Rahul's genuine desire to spend time with her. She pushed aside the doubts; she cared about this man and would not let go of this great opportunity to be with him to know him better.

'It's a great idea!' she said finally, her face reflecting her determination and happiness.

'Are you sure... I mean... That's great,' Rahul said happily, before adding, 'It's done then. Two days of work and two days we shall have fun. We will have a great time holidaying together.'

'I've never been to Hong Kong.'

'We will have a blast,' Rahul added, and then looked at her with a twinkle in his eyes. He added, 'I am so glad you agreed to this, Simran. We will get to spend a lot of time together and really get to know each other better.'

Simran wanted to throw her arms around him, but she checked herself. He had never initiated any physical contact, except the hugs when he left her place after his visits.

Later, when Simran was alone, she wondered how Rahul had just envisioned this impulsive trip; were they just going on a holiday as friends or did this mean a deeper commitment at another level. Once again, she stopped her thoughts from overpowering the preparations she would need to make. She decided to just go with the flow and see how things worked out.

Simran decided not to tell Ruby and Madhu. Not that she feared admonishment, but she did not want to field too many questions from them. She needed to take this step with Rahul to understand how important this relationship was for her. From then onwards, whenever Rahul came over, she tried to examine his words and expressions carefully to understand whether he was as eager about the trip as she was. But his ready smiles and discussions on their itinerary gave nothing away.

The day finally arrived.

Their flight was at half past three in the morning. He called her the evening before.

'Would you mind getting to the airport on your own? Sonia and the kids want to drop me to the airport,' he said apologetically. 'I have arranged for a cab to fetch you.'

'No problem. I can get to the airport on my own; I will ask my taxi stand to send a cab.'

'No, I have arranged for a cab. See you at the check-in counter. Wait for me in case I am late.'

'Ok, see you there.' She didn't want to argue over a cab.

Simran disconnected the call. She had been sitting in front of the mirror brushing her hair. She looked at her reflection intently. Were these lines of worry on her forehead? Of course, it was natural for Rahul's family to want to drop him at the airport when he was leaving for an international trip. *She* was the *outsider. Was she doing the right thing?* The thought almost gave her a panic attack. She wanted to call Rahul and drop the idea of travelling with him. But she pulled herself together. This decision, of going with him, was an important one for her, more so because she wanted to understand her, and Rahul's commitment towards this relationship. She had been waiting for this day and she was not going to analyse things unnecessarily. Of course, she was a tad confused, but she would be strong enough to stick to her decision.

They met at the check-in counter, rolled through immigration and boarded the aircraft. Rahul settled down with his drinks. Simran was a bundle of nerves; how she wished she could enjoy her drinks too. Knocking back a few stiff ones was the call of the hour. They chatted for a while till she was overpowered by sleep. The last thought on her mind, before she drifted off, was that it would have been comforting had Rahul reached out to hold her hand; it would have eased her mind.

CHAPTER 5

Landing in Hong Kong, they quickly passed through customs and took a taxi to the Grand Hyatt.

Simran looked around at the busy streets. It was her first trip to Hong Kong. She had Rahul as her guide and was determined to keep every experience close to her heart.

The receptionist at the hotel asked, 'Sir, twin beds or a double bed?'

Simran moved away, pretending she hadn't heard the question. She wanted to see how Rahul would respond; his decision would set the precedent for the rest of the trip and give her an idea of what he would be expecting.

He gave her a sideway glance and she avoided eye contact and tried to ensure that her expression would not give away her anticipation.

Rahul told the receptionist, 'We would require two rooms with a double bed in each please.'

Simran heard and was a bit disappointed. She didn't know how to interpret Rahul's decision of taking two rooms. *But then...why had Rahul asked for a double bed in each? What was going on in his mind? Did the night have any surprises in store?* She didn't have any answers and Rahul was very reticent on the way to the room.

Rahul had requested for adjoining rooms, which were quite spacious. Both went inside their respective rooms, and discovered the connecting door. Rahul opened the connecting door to Simran's room and entered. However, he made no effort to hold her hand or come closer. Once again Simran was a bit disappointed.

Rahul said suddenly, 'I thought you would be comfortable with a double bed in your own space... I didn't want to disappoint you,' he said and smiled at her mischievously.

Was this a test of some sort? Simran wondered. How was he expecting her to respond?

'Of course! A double bed is any day...more comfortable,' she responded inanely. 'Please don't take it amiss but I'll be more comfortable paying my own bills.'

Simran noticed his face visibly relax. He had thrown the ball in her court! While planning this trip, he had been telling himself repeatedly that he wanted to romance her in Hong Kong. It was time their relationship moved on to the next level but he had decided to wait. He wanted the moment to be absolutely perfect.

They spent the next hour chatting over coffee in Simran's room. He told her about the city and its various attractions and promised to take her around. He had to leave for a meeting. She was disappointed but consoled herself with the thought that they would have enough time to spend with each other later. He promised to be back soon.

Simran unpacked for both of them. She stepped into the shower and took her time to undress. *Why am I being so moody? Why am I getting disturbed that he isn't making any advances? Do I want to get intimate? It's been time since me and...* Her thoughts trailed off to her last physical encounter with her now ex-husband. The passion had died a slow death. That had been years ago. She looked into the mirror while taking a shower. *Did her body yearn for it? Did she yearn for it? Was she absolutely confident of taking this relationship to the next level?* Somewhere inside her mind, she heard a faint 'yes'. Her carnal desires had resurfaced. They were after all lying dormant in Delhi.

She stepped out of the hotel, strolling through the streets aimlessly. After a couple of hours she returned to the hotel; tired and wanted to just hit the bed. She had barely dozed off when she heard a knock.

'Please come back later,' she shouted irritably, deciding that whoever it was could be of no importance.

The knocking persisted.

Was Rahul back early? She thought and jumped out of the bed to open the door. It was him.

'Hey! You locked my room as well. Did I wake you up?'

'How are you back so early?' she said, happy to see him.

'Wanted to be with you madamé, what would you like to do?'

She had no answers.

'We could step out and walk around the streets,' he suggested.

Simran was confused by this suggestion. *Why would he want to go out for coffee instead of cosying up in the hotel?* But it also reassured her that she had not chosen a completely wrong person to fall for and that he would not take undue advantage of her.

They stepped out into Hong Kong's busy streets. Simran revelled in the hustle and bustle of the high street. Since she had more or less accepted Rahul as part of her life, she savoured the privilege of romancing him freely under the open skies of Hong Kong, and her inner voice repeatedly affirming that this was the man for her. She was delighted to discover that he was attentive and fun-loving too. They tried out the street food; just like she did in Delhi and other cities she travelled to.

'Rahul, the best way to experience a place is through its food, especially street food,' Simran said.

'You mean even try this strange looking stuff that you can't recognise,' Rahul replied, spooning the bowl that had been placed before him.

'Especially the things that you have never seen before,' Simran stressed on what she said and laughed.

She was very happy with these shared moments and when Rahul reached out to hold her hand she closed her fingers around his. Later, as they walked back to the hotel, Rahul put his arms around her and pulled her closer. Simran cherished this comforting feeling.

It was well after 11:30 pm when they finally reached the hotel, totally exhausted.

'Do you want to go to one of the nightclubs?' Rahul asked.

'I don't mind, if you want to, but I am really tired. Let's save it for tomorrow.'

'You are right. Even I am bushed! Tomorrow for sure; the nightlife is really great in this city.'

Rahul and she walked into the hotel hand-in-hand, unburdened by the fear that somebody might see them together. It was all like a dream. She was in love after a very long time. The feeling was euphoric. She was no longer confused. This was the man she wanted.

Once in her room, Simran decided to freshen up. Rahul switched on the television. As she pondered over what to wear to bed, she knew that this trip was a major step; it was a commitment to the kind of life she could envision for them together. She had been apprehensive right after she had promised to accompany him, but her feelings for him had helped her tide over her fears. He was decent; something that had been apparent to her throughout the day today, when he had taken her around the city. Not once had he done anything to make her feel uncomfortable. But she admitted that she was nervous about what to expect from him now.

A sudden knock made her realise that she had been in the washroom longer than she had intended to. Appalled at her silliness, she quickly slipped into her nightshirt and stepped out.

'The bed is much more comfortable than the bathtub, Simran,' Rahul joked when he noticed her apologetic look. He added, 'I came over to ask if you would like to pop a bottle of champagne...to us?'

'Sure,' Simran answered with a broad smile.

She got into her bed. Her room was dimly lit with just one light on near the doorway.

Rahul went back to his room to get the bubbly. Simran thought how surreal everything was. Her thoughts sailed through the first time she had met Rahul, and the unexplained chemistry she had experienced when they laughed together on the way to see his paintings and how they had drifted into this relationship, spending all their free time with each other. *When did love happen?* And now, she had travelled to another country with him without informing her family or friends. *Had she been impulsive? Was she taking a risk?* She panicked.

'Are you ok Simran?' Rahul's voice cut into her fears. 'You look preoccupied.' He was standing on the other side of the bed and looking at her intently.

Rahul handed her the bubbly and held his own glass up for a toast, 'To us.'

'For us,' Simran smiled.

Rahul got into Simran's bed, on the other side. As they sipped their champagne, they planned their itinerary for the next day. Rahul told Simran about the various sight-seeing places and his earlier trips to the country. They both drained their glasses at the same time.

'Should I get you some more?' Rahul asked.

'We have a long day tomorrow; I think we should call it a day,' Simran smiled.

Rahul reached out to hold Simran's hand. Giving it a light squeeze, he said, 'I had a great day today. Thanks so much.' He looked into her eyes and Simran wished the moment would continue for eternity. After a pause, he abruptly said, 'Let's sleep.'

'Yes, I am so tired. Lots to see and do tomorrow,' Simran said, as she lay down flat on her back. She could sense that Rahul was looking at her.

'Simran, please relax... We are friends. Trust me... Just relax and go to sleep,' he said after a short while.

You are not a gawky teenager for heaven sake, Simran chided herself! She had taken the decision to come here and she was not going to get cold feet over taking their relationship further.

'I am ok, Rahul. Just takes me a while to get used to a new bed,' she smiled and reassured him, unable to think of a better excuse.

'Let us keep the light on. Would that be ok with you?' Rahul asked, and she nodded in agreement.

After sometime he reached out for Simran's hand under the duvet and asked if he could hold her and Simran agreed. She wanted to move past the awkwardness; to let go of all inhibitions. Her smile was all the encouragement he needed.

What followed was beautiful. They discovered each other with all their senses; exploring their passion for each other. The fervour between them was enigmatic and untamed. For Simran, the physical union only intensified and strengthened her love for Rahul. It didn't feel like just a physical union but actually seemed like an expression of their feelings for each other, which was one of love.

She didn't want this night to end. It would be etched in her mind forever. *He is the one*, she told herself repeatedly. She knew that she would love this man till eternity. They made love that night.

Simran saw the sky turn orangish-blue and wanted to coax him out of bed and see the sunrise cuddled in his tight embrace, but sleep was overtaking her, so she wrapped herself in his arms and fell asleep. As they drifted off to sleep, Rahul whispered in her ear, 'I love you...and I haven't felt this way with any other woman before.'

'I love you too and I have never felt like this about any man ever in my life,' Simran responded.

Simran couldn't have slept more than a couple of hours, when the alarm went off. She was still in a state of rapture, recounting the previous night's experience. She was happy to gaze at Rahul's smiling face. As she moved to get up, Rahul rolled over to her, pushed her duvet away and lay on top of her, kissing her eyes one at a time. She put her arms around him.

'You have cast a spell on me,' he said, gazing into her eyes.

She smiled and smoothed the hair on his forehead.

'Sorry, I had to set the alarm. I have to go for a meeting at 10. Should I order some tea?'

Simran nodded, dying for her morning cuppa.

When Rahul left a short while later, she drifted back to sleep, wanting to prolong the feeling of a newfound contentment.

She was woken up with Rahul kissing her cheek and caressing her hair. 'Get up, sleeping beauty.'

Simran felt guilty for enjoying the comforts of her bed while he had been away, working.

'I'm done with work, let's step out and party,' he said enthusiastically.

There was so much to do in Hong Kong that time just flew by. They went to the Victoria Harbour for an evening cruise; the place captured the local flavour completely.

Mountains surrounded the harbour from all sides, as a natural shield from the typhoons which hit the city every summer. The couple sat at the harbour front soaking up the night breeze. The harbour was the city's heart and one of the world's most awesome urban landscapes. Simran and Rahul sat there in absolute silence taking in the enchantment of their surroundings; there was no urge to talk as they sat listening to the sound of the sea and watching the stunning skyline and the dazzling neon cityscape merging to become one.

The beauty of the surroundings seemed to reflect the joy in Simran's heart as she sat cuddled in Rahul's arms. She captured every moment in her heart and confessed to herself that till now she had never understood how being in love could be so beautiful.

Like all tourists, they wanted to explore Hong Kong's various attractions. On the other days, after Rahul finished his work, they decided to ride on the Ding-Ding Tram. The tram line stretched from Kennedy Town to Shaun Kei, with seven stops in-between. The tram also took them to the Causeway Bay—a Mecca for the fashionistas and the gourmands. They hopped off and spent a few hours shopping and relishing the delicacies. Rahul would pull her into the stores and compel her to buy clothes of his choice. Shopping was something that didn't interest Simran much. She loved Chinese food and happily stuffed her face with whatever fascinated her. Rahul was amused at how she could not resist what was on offer although it was difficult for her to put another morsel into her mouth. Clubbing too was not Simran's cup of tea. However, it was an opportunity she didn't want to miss. So they decided to take a quick trip to the local clubs before returning to the hotel.

The two walked aimlessly for hours, hand-in-hand; completely oblivious to the world, away from home and all things familiar. They talked for hours; about each other, their families and children. Rahul conceded that he was in a meaningless marriage. Simran respected his candour. She wasn't jealous of Sonia. Her only desire was to be loved sincerely by Rahul. She was single and had the liberty to lead her life the way she wanted to. The word *home-breaker* did not play on her conscience even once. She firmly believed that a third person did not have the power to destroy a long-standing relationship. In Rahul's own words, his marriage to Sonia had not grown, *had it not*, Simran asked herself.

Rahul filled a void in Simran's life and for that she was grateful. Rahul himself had never been happier. She had rekindled his zest for romance; he wanted to do things he hadn't done in years—like watch a movie holding hands; or maybe go for long walks in parks amidst the beauty of the gardens and butterflies. It had been years since he had gone for a candle-light dinner or even dancing. He now felt blessed. He felt happy knowing he loved her and that she loved him too.

Their time in Hong Kong soon drew to a close.

'I will call you as soon as I get to Delhi. Enjoy Chennai,' Rahul said as they parted with each other at the airport.

Simran hugged him, saying, 'I will really miss you. I feel terrible that we can't go back together.'

'Change your ticket and come back to Delhi with me,' he coaxed.

'You know I can't. But I wish you were coming too,' she said with a smile.

They bid adieu, with each moving on to catch their respective flights. As Simran sat alone in the airport lounge, she went through the last four days of togetherness with Rahul. *Would she be able to go back to a life where he was not there with her all the time?* She felt a deep yearning to see him and hear his voice. He was in the same airport but they could not see each other; much the same way when they would be living in the same city but not be able to see each other when she wanted. She chastised herself for her childish longings, reminding herself that she was aware of the complexities of their relationship. The days in Hong Kong were far removed from the reality of their lives. And she would be happy and content if she accepted that.

CHAPTER 6

Simran would be seeing Karishma after six weeks. It was a happy reunion between a mother and her daughter. Karishma was overjoyed to see the things her mother had brought for her.

Simran watched her daughter as she got busy with the gifts. *Would she ever be able to tell Karishma about Rahul?* She was surprisingly mature for her age, accepting the fact that her father would no longer be a part of her life.

Simran had been extremely vigilant after her divorce, making sure that Karishma felt protected, despite losing a *conventional* home. Her daughter was her lifeline. She remembered how she had seen her ex-husband negotiating for Karishma's finances, in cold business terms. He threatened to sue her for child custody and snatch Karishma if she even thought of asking for child maintenance. Karishma was living in Chennai, safe and secure; Simran didn't want her uprooted. She and her family felt the child would be better looked after if she was with her grandparents. Asking for anything would mean dragging the child in and out of court for years.

Subjecting a little girl to cross examination in court was unthinkable. Determined not to get into any kind of *arrangement* with him, she had signed on the dotted line, for no alimony or child maintenance, picked up Karishma in her arms and walked out. There would never be a price tag for her little baby. There was no way she was going to let her daughter come under the influence of an irresponsible father like her ex-husband. It was a good decision. He never ever looked over his shoulder, or enquired if the child was ok. Luckily, her family had stood by Karishma and her during such tough times; the child had escaped without having to go through a traumatic experience. All Simran wanted was a stable home for her, which her grandparents were adequately providing.

The days away from Rahul would also give her the opportunity to analyse her relationship with him. Was Rahul treating Simran as a temporary arrangement to escape his boring marriage? Would he call her in Chennai? The complications of getting involved with a married man were building insecurities. She told herself that in Hong Kong, they only had each other and no one else. Rahul had measured up to all her expectations. But this was reality–that he had a wife and a family to return to. These thoughts combined into a serious concern for her, and her mother too pointed out that she was distracted. Simran tried to engage in conversation with each of them but her mind refused to be at rest. She needed some answers.

She had been home for less than a couple of hours when Rahul called.

He caught the strain in her voice, 'What's the matter, are you unwell?'

'No, just a wee bit tired...and the excitement of being with my family. My mother can't stop talking, she wants all the updates. I think I need some sleep.'

'Sleep well dear, since I'm not around to bother you,' she could sense his smile. 'When is a good time to call you?' he asked.

'I don't want my family to know about us now. So I will call you when I can talk,' she responded, before disconnecting.

Simran felt awful, she had never ever hidden anything from her family before. She stood looking out of the window at the clean and non-cluttered streets of Besant Nagar, with the green trees creating small islands of shadow–under which vegetable vendors had parked their carts–and lending the area a tranquil aura. Simran took a deep breath taking in the peaceful environs. The close proximity to her parents lent a great sense of comfort to her troubled mind. *Did she not go to Delhi to find the same peace of mind; more so after the last few acrimonious years of her marriage?* But now, she was making her life more complicated than before, thanks to her relationship with a married man.

Yes, she was worried, but the thought of Rahul also brought a smile to her lips. She felt like a queen when she was with him. She really had no reason to complain, except for that niggling doubt at the back of her mind–*Rahul was a married man and he had other commitments.* What kind of a future could she envision with him?

She called him that evening.

'I am missing you,' she said.

'That's great, because I was missing you too. I'm so happy to have you in my life,' he replied.

'Rahul, I have a question,' she got directly to the point, 'where are we heading?'

The questions that had been plaguing her mind all afternoon surfaced again. She had to ask him.

'What a ridiculous question? We are heading where people in love head. Bliss!' he said and chuckled. Then he continued, 'You mean the world to me. I fell for you the moment I saw you at my house. I understand I am married, but loving you is my prerogative and no one can stop that, not even my family. Only you can when you tire of me, but I am not giving you that option.'

Simran could visualise the intensity on his face as he uttered these words. Perhaps, she was jumping the gun. They had only taken a trip together. *Could she really demand an undying commitment? But then, did she want that kind of commitment at this stage of her life?* She was an emotional person and her confusion was not helping her either.

He seemed to sense that something was bothering her.

'Enjoy your time with your daughter and parents. I will see you at the airport when you return. Don't burden your mind with unnecessary worries,' he said. They talked for a few minutes more and disconnected.

Simran scolded herself for almost forcefully steering her thoughts into this confusion. There was really no need to expect anything definite now; both from Rahul and her own mind. She would just go with the flow. She was mature enough to handle whatever came her way.

Simran spoke to Rahul every day for the next couple of weeks; ensuring that she did not invite much curiosity from her parents and her daughter. The weeks just flew and by the time she headed back to the airport she felt sorry to leave the family behind. Parting with them was always arduous.

Rahul kept his promise and was at the airport to receive her. She was thrilled and his face mirrored the same response. They both rushed to each other but then she suddenly stopped herself; this was Delhi. She had to be careful. But Rahul grabbed her hand and walked her to his car.

'Hope you won't be going off again. I really missed you,' he said after they had left the airport.

Simran leaned across and kissed him on his cheek, 'Rahul, I too missed you a lot.'

'It's strange but in such a short span of time you have come to mean so much to me. Where were you all these years?' he reached out to hold her hand.

She laughed, 'I really have to thank Madhu for coercing me to go to your house.'

'Did you have a good trip? You look relaxed.'

'Yes, I love being with my family, I especially cherish the time with Karishma. Rahul, I have been thinking...I truly enjoyed our trip and it was my decision to go with you. I will be happy for us to remain just friends. I don't want you to get into anything more than this without being sure of what you truly want.'

He interrupted her, 'Simran, I have waited a really long time for you to come back. Can we discuss whatever has been bothering you later?'

They had reached Simran's place by then.

They reached home and fell into each other's arms. All her misgivings forgotten, she let herself drown in the intense feelings he aroused in her. She admitted that she too had craved for a physical reunion.

Later, she watched the sky changing colour from orange to grey, while Rahul dozed off. The growing darkness outside mirrored the thoughts she had tried hard to keep at bay. Rahul knew that something had been bothering her, yet chose not to ask her about it. He was smart and knew excessive probing would mean encouraging her to emote. Did this augur well for their future? That is, if they had one together, Simran wondered? Her weakness for this man made her inadequate to have the strength to reason sensibly with him or herself. But then she brushed these doubts aside, as she remembered the joy on his face at the airport. He had been genuinely happy to see her. Her fears could wait, she was going to enjoy the present with him. That was the only thing that mattered to her now.

CHAPTER 7

The trip to Hong Kong became the precursor of their lives together; Simran would now accompany him on all his business trips. They would anxiously wait for these *holidays*. At times, Rahul would engineer trips so that they could get away together; enjoying each others' company away from the claustrophobic life of Delhi.

He would pick her up on the way to the airport every time. Simran liked his protectiveness; it was endearing. Their trips to Düsseldorf, Germany, were particularly memorable. Rahul loved Düsseldorf when it snowed and Simran dreaded winters.

However their first winter together in Düsseldorf, felt different for Simran. It was enchanting. She snuggled into her woollen top coat, put on her gloves, and pulled down her woollen cap to cover most of her face as she disembarked from the aircraft at Düsseldorf airport. Rahul had brazenly just worn a woollen jacket to tackle the –5°C temperature outside. Five seconds later his teeth were chattering. Finally they snuggled into her coat!

During the trip, one particular day, she lost her way on the highway after visiting a friend in the suburbs. She found herself driving up and down, for two hours, till the police helped her to find the hotel in which she was staying.

She walked into the lobby and saw Rahul sitting on the sofa, ashen-faced, staring at the entrance door. The minute he saw her, he ran and grabbed her. He was shaking from head to foot and his eyes were moist. 'What happened? Why didn't you call me? I have been sitting on this sofa for two hours. You are always so punctual; I was really frightened. If you hadn't returned in the next 10 minutes I would have called the police. I just didn't know what to do,' he rattled on and on, not giving her a chance to reply.

'I am fine, just calm down, and relax.'

He just embraced her, 'I thought of the worst; these highways are very treacherous.'

She assured him that she was absolutely fine and explained why she had got delayed. Her heart danced at the thought that he cared so much about her.

Rahul worked long hours and Simran loved waiting for him, even though he would insist that she go shopping. Simran did not enjoy shopping; she preferred going for a swim or to the health club in the hotel or just watching a movie in bed, with chips and a can of soft drink.

At times she did this mischievously just to induce guilt, so that he would return earlier than usual. It worked most of the time. Evenings were romantic; usually spent in long walks or over hot cups of coffee in a quaint café to beat the cold outside, or pizza meals at a little pizza place, close to the hotel they usually stayed in. They avoided crowded places; were just happy in each other's company. They visited Düsseldorf several times; but being with Rahul made each trip special for Simran. They managed to pack in a lot in the few days of each trip to the city.

~

Back home it was soon time to celebrate the New Year. Simran knew that as much as she wanted, it would be unfair to demand that Rahul spend time with her this New Year. His family, especially his children, would expect him to be with them. Once again, this made Simran aware that she was an *outsider* and not an integral part of Rahul's family, or for that matter, his public life; he had already decided that they would not go out together in Delhi. This did rattle her and make her more insecure, but she brushed it under the carpet every time. Avoiding confrontations was a deliberate exercise that was turning into a habit.

Simran's friends chose the Golf Club to celebrate New Year's Eve. Rahul convinced his friends to choose the same venue. Simran had to live with the fact that Sonia would be part of the group but was happy with the thought that at least she would be able to see him.

The club was chock-a-block, much more crowded than what they had expected. They kept looking for each other. Simran avoided calling him knowing that he was with his wife. She was edgy and it was almost midnight—with just 10 minutes to go—when she spotted him. They exchanged a warm smile from a distance, the sea of people between them. She had almost raised her hand to wave out to him but retracted remembering that she hadn't told Madhu and Ruby that she and Rahul had become good friends, or probably, even more than that. These little incidents left Simran unsettled, constricting her vivacious nature and making her feel claustrophobic. It always reiterated the fact that Rahul was a much-married man.

Rahul began to walk towards her. They looked at each other as he started moving towards her group. He had almost reached her when the crowd began the countdown to midnight. When the clock finally struck 12, Simran saw Rahul standing right in front of her.

'I love you,' he whispered, as he caught her momentarily in a hug. People around them were busy wishing each other *'Happy New Year'* and no one noticed them.

'You are crazy,' chuckled Simran as she hugged him, taking in the warmth of his presence.

'Only for you,' Rahul responded.

He let go of her and she noticed that he was looking behind her. She turned to find Madhu and Ruby close by.

'I must go back to my friends,' Rahul told them after he had wished them and soon disappeared into the crowd.

Simran thought to herself that it was surely providence that had ensured that they could be with each other on this occasion.

'We should have asked Rahul to join us with his friends,' Madhu piped in later.

'Let's not be intrusive, he's with his own gang,' Simran said immediately. She was very uncomfortable at the probability that Madhu or Ruby might invite Rahul and his companions to their table.

She added, 'Besides, there is no place at our table.'

'Big deal! It's New Year. We'll make place; the more the merrier,' Ruby said enthusiastically.

'Let it be Ruby,' Simran said again.

Ruby looked at her strangely and shrugged her shoulders.

Simran didn't want to be a hypocrite; she wanted to maintain distance from Sonia.

~

Soon after the New Year, it was celebration time again. It was Rahul's 40th birthday and he was planning a big party the day before the actual date. Simran and Rahul discussed it in detail but he didn't know how to invite her. Madhu and Ruby were acquaintances of his mother and even if he did invite them (he had no plans of doing that) how could he invite Simran when it was known that he had met her only once. She decided it was best for her to stay away. The current arrangement between them worked just fine, she thought. The certainty of Rahul missing her on his birthday celebrations gave Simran a feeling of satisfaction. She didn't want to ruin his big day by making a hue and cry about this.

He dropped by on his way from work and insisted that she should attend his party. But she stuck to her decision.

'Enjoy yourself and I hope you miss me a lot,' she told him with a smile. While leaving, he embraced her like he was never going to let her go.

Although she had rationalised everything in her mind, she felt excluded from this momentous occasion in his life. Throughout the evening she fought the desire to call him. What if he was not in a position to take her call? She would feel more horrid then. She tried to force herself to sleep but it eluded her. Simran had been tossing and turning for a long time when the phone rang, piercing the silence of her dark bedroom.

It was Rahul.

'Hi! I want you to be the first to wish me.'

'Is it midnight already? Where are you?'

'In the washroom,' he chuckled, and added, 'Come on, aren't you going to wish me?'

'Happy birthday, Rahul. I really love you. I wish I could hug you now,' Simran said, in a low voice, sounding upset. 'I wanted to be with you on your special day. Maybe...next year,' her eyes misted over. Spending time with someone you love, especially so on their special occasions, was something taken for granted. This inability was what was gnawing at her mind.

'Good idea,' he said, trying to cheer her up.

She quickly asked, 'How is it going? Are you having a good time?'

'Frankly, I wish I hadn't organised this party. I am just aimlessly going from guest to guest. What's the point when I am not enjoying myself and my heart is with you?'

'Listen, you must get back, everyone must be looking for you,' Simran said.

'What can I do if I suddenly have a bad stomach; blame the caterers,' he joked, and they both laughed.

Rahul later told her that Sonia had kept a sour face the rest of the evening after he returned to the party; she had obviously noticed that he was not around at midnight. 'I just can't deal with a sulky person.'

Simran did not comment on this, but wondered if Sonia was growing suspicious. It was possible; after all she shared the roof with him. The possibility did not however alarm her. For Simran, the feeling of alienation was more pronounced now after Rahul's birthday bash. This feeling provoked her to re-evaluate her position in his life. *For how long am I going to be his dark secret?*

Simran's only outing with Rahul, when in Delhi, was an occasional movie or going for long drives or listening to music. Rahul insisted that they enter the theatre after the movie started and leave before the film credits started rolling. Added to that, he insisted that they sit in the stalls; nobody from their circle of acquaintances was likely to watch a movie by sitting there, right at front. Their love story had many rules which did make her very unhappy and uncomfortable at times.

Over time, Rahul became the pivot of Simran's life. She planned her days around him and his phone calls and kept him informed about all that was happening in her life, but never demanding that he do the same. And when together, they were like two people who seemed to have missed out on the opportunity to romance in their adolescent days.

With every passing day Simran's love for Rahul swelled like an incoming tide. She accepted that their love story had limitations. Unlike most other couples in love, they seldom had differences.

~

It was more than a couple of years now since Simran had been with Rahul. They were happy with the pattern their lives had fallen into. Simran now had her work which took up a great deal of her day. She had been working with an export house for a few months and had managed to learn everything about the manufacturing side of the business. She wanted to get into the financial side before she could start off on her own. Her ultimate goal was to have her own factory and work independantly. She had her hobbies too–she loved going to the club to swim in the summer months; she was passionate about tennis; she loved watching movies every weekend; and she enjoyed singing and had her music teacher come over twice a week. She caught up with the stock market over the weekends and had managed to sell a small plot of land she owned and was now looking to buy another flat in Gurgaon. Life was busy.

As they could not be seen socialising together, Simran had even distanced herself from her friends; in fact, had done so without a thought as Rahul had become the reason for her happiness. Over time, she had become very dependent on him emotionally. This, she acknowledged, made her feel lonely, insecure and vulnerable.

CHAPTER 8

The gang of girls had been invited to Ruby's place for lunch. A couple of other friends were also present apart from Simran and Madhu.

'I have a surprise for all of you,' Ruby said excitedly.

Simran could guess what the surprise might be. She had never seen Ruby looking happier. But she, along with the others, waited for Ruby's surprise.

'Anil and I have decided to get married, but in sometime, not immediately.'

The friends screamed in chorus.

'Whenever we plan the engagement, each one of you, will have a special duty. Anil is buying me a gift tomorrow, as he wants to seal this news with something special. The engagement ring can wait,' Ruby announced.

'How many carats?' her friend Sharmila asked cheekily.

'I don't care. It can be a rubber band for all I care. I love him and want to be with him, that's all that matters,' Ruby responded happily.

Everyone in the room burst out laughing. 'Rubber band, really!,' everyone repeated together. This one was a truly original line!

'We have enough time to prepare,' Sharmila said.

'Yes, we do. Don't worry. Each one will get a specific job,' Madhu said.

'I know I can leave it to you Simran to look out for a caterer and take care of the décor,' Ruby said confidently.

The group got busy planning Ruby's happy day.

~

Amidst this euphoria surrounding Ruby's engagement, the most unexpected thing occurred. Simran opened the front door of her house one day to find Madhu; dishevelled and in tears.

A horrified Simran took her into the house. Madhu could hardly talk; she was crying bitterly, gasping for breath before every sentence.

'My god, what happened?' Simran went to hug Madhu, trying to decipher the words she uttered between her wailing.

'My...my world...has...collapsed... Destroyed...my life is destroyed... What will I do... What will I do now?' Madhu rambled.

Simran was terrified, 'For god's sake, speak coherently. Are the girls alright?'

'Raghav... He is having an affair with Radha. I caught them together...and the children now know about it,' Madhu finally blurted out.

'Don't be silly. Get a grip on yourself, Madhu. Have you lost your marbles,' Simran said.

'It is true!' Madhu yelled back.

It was Simran's turn to be stunned. Madhu and Raghav were the perfect couple. They and their two beautiful daughters were the epitome of a happy family. *There surely was some misunderstanding* she told herself. Radha was their close family friend.

'Calm down and tell me what happened.'

Madhu was trembling.

'Radha had no family in Delhi. I felt sorry for her and thought it would be good if she spent time at our place, instead of being alone at home. I couldn't imagine Raghav doing this to me...behind my back,' Madhu said, in between heaving sobs.

'And...' Simran prompted, patiently listening and hanging on to each and everything that Madhu said.

'I saw them being friendly to each other, but I never suspected something like this would happen... We have been married for 18 years... How could Raghav do this to us?'

'Are you sure?' Simran still couldn't believe her ears.

'Damn it! I caught them together,' Madhu shouted.

'Ok, ok... Sorry... Carry on...it's just that I can't believe this.'

'I got back early this afternoon after the school parent-teacher's meeting and the bedroom door was locked. I knocked and there was no response. I waited and knocked again. Raghav eventually opened the door saying that he had been asleep. Raghav never locks the bedroom door; it did seem a bit strange. And the next moment I heard a mobile ring in the balcony. I thought Raghav must have forgotten his phone there. But then the ringing stopped. I saw Raghav's face freeze. He turned towards the balcony but I got there before him. Radha was standing there with her cell phone in her hand. It didn't take me long to put the pieces together. He had obviously thought he would let her slip out when I stepped into the washroom.'

'Oh my god!' Simran exclaimed in horror.

Madhu continued, 'I was so shocked that for a while I just stood there, unable to react. Then I could not hold back my anger and disgust. The man had the audacity to come up with excuses; as though I hadn't seen anything. By then the girls had also returned from school. They ran into our bedroom at our raised voices and witnessed the entire drama. Radha, in the meanwhile, had run out of the house. Since then, my home has been a battlefield.'

'What does Raghav have to say in his defence?' Simran asked.

'He finally ran out of excuses to defend himself. He wants a divorce,' Madhu by now had calmed down considerably. She added, 'He now wants his freedom. I am financially dependent on him, my kids have not completed their education and I don't even have a roof over my head... What a mess. What do I do now?'

'What about the girls? What do they have to say?'

'They are at loggerheads with their father. After all, they are teenagers and can understand everything.'

Simran could not fathom how Madhu's world could have collapsed. She had always been the perfect homemaker; watching over the needs of her children and Raghav. Eighteen years of marriage and what did that amount to? Raghav had thrown away everything that they had built up over these years.

Madhu left after a while. Simran assured her that Ruby and she would visit her the next day. She made Madhu promise that she would not give in to rage and abuse, as she had earlier, no matter how Raghav might try to provoke her. It was an ugly situation and she definitely should not make it uglier.

Alone in the house, concern for Madhu and her friend's future overwhelmed Simran. She and Ruby had to ensure that Madhu would not go into pieces over this. She would have to agree to the divorce; what was the point in hanging onto a marriage when your spouse cared for somebody else. Simran wondered how Radha could agree to be the *other* woman in Raghav's life.

The other woman? Simran asked herself. Could she really judge a situation like this? But Rahul was not going to end his marriage. And Sonia was in a stronger financial position; her family was there to support her. Madhu did not have anybody, except her sister. *What really justified an extra-marital affair? Did anybody else deserve to be cheated on, like how Raghav did with Madhu...or as Rahul was doing in the case of his marriage...*she reminded herself quietly?

'Raghav is having an affair with Madhu's friend and now wants a divorce,' Simran broke the news to Rahul that evening. 'These guys have been married for 18 long years. Suddenly he wants to be out. She has no home, where will she go?'

Rahul was strangely distant in his response.

'Mind your own business and leave it to Raghav to sort out his domestic issues.'

'Madhu is my friend and she expects me to stand by her and I will Rahul, come what may.'

'Well then do what you like, but leave me out of this.'

Simran was taken aback! She was not asking him to go and rough up Raghav for heaven's sake. She only wanted him to extend his sympathies to Madhu; she was also his friend. But Rahul obviously did not share her sentiments. Was he afraid that this might bring their relationship into public glare?

But there was no chance of that happening, was there? For the first time, she came face to face with Rahul, who could completely cut himself off from a situation that did not concern him directly.

When Rahul went home that evening he was visibly disturbed... *The last thing I need is something like this to happen so close to home*, he thought. *This is what is happening in my life with Simran and Sonia.*

Madhu's life, in the meanwhile, had taken a deplorable turn. Raghav packed and left the house one morning, without informing her. They had been living in a rented house and now she had no money, no job and no support system. He wouldn't take her calls or reply to her messages. Madhu was terrified at the turn of events. She decided to go over to his office where his indifference shattered her further; he was obviously not willing to take her responsibility anymore. When Madhu asked what would happen to their daughters, Raghav was evasive and did not give any definite answers.

'I have made a huge mistake by trusting Raghav blindly,' Madhu repeated whenever she was with her friends.

Raghav and Madhu had started dating when she was just 16 years old; she had loved him practically all her life. She had lost her father when she was very young and Raghav had been her world. Her friends were shocked and outraged that he had so easily betrayed the implicit trust of so many years of friendship and marriage. However, the friends gave a patient ear to Madhu's emotional outburst from time to time, given her situation. Ruby even offered to talk to Raghav, as a mediator, but Madhu vetoed it saying that he might be rude and offensive.

The situation with Madhu would often compel Simran to introspect. *Was Rahul any different from Raghav? More importantly, was she any different from Radha?* The only difference was that Rahul was not asking Sonia for a divorce. Now with Madhu's predicament right before her, she began to question many of the decisions she had been making in her life. Love had its own place; yes she was compatible with Rahul, something which was severely missing in her own marriage. It wasn't easy for her to live with someone suffering with mood swings and depression. Now with Madhu's problem staring at her in the face, she felt awkward to think of her own relationship with Rahul. She had never stopped to think things through. She was in love, emotionally dependent and weak-kneed to do something about it. She had to talk to Rahul seriously.

'If Madhu's marriage can break down, then anything is possible,' Simran wondered aloud, as the three friends met at her place one day.

'Why doesn't he make provisions for the girls? He has a responsibility towards his daughters at least,' Ruby remarked.

'I can't agree to the Rs 30 lakhs that he is offering. How will that take care of our expenses and the education of my kids?'

Madhu was in tears again.

'My daughters have to be educated. They have to be financially independent and live with dignity. I will not have them dependent on anyone ever. What a terrible way to learn a lesson,' Madhu lamented.

'You think he might come back and apologise one day?' Ruby asked.

'I don't want him back,' Madhu said firmly. 'I might have to fend for myself, and that's alright; but it definitely won't be enough for my daughters to get a standard education and for their further studies.'

Simran and Ruby smiled at each other and gave Madhu a hug. They each wondered if Madhu had the willpower to keep him at arm's length or would she give in. She was too vulnerable as far as Raghav was concerned. Or would Madhu rise like the phoenix and fly again?

Simran and Ruby were determined that they would do everything they could to protect Madhu...even if she and Raghav reconciled in the distant future.

CHAPTER 9

In the meanwhile, cracks began to appear in Rahul and Simran's near-perfect equation. He wanted her closeted in her boudoir alienating herself from her friends. With Madhu's circumstances too close for comfort, he objected to Madhu and Simran meeting often. He knew Simran's empathy for Madhu would not espouse what Raghav was putting her through. Simran often brought up their topic leading to fierce arguments; he didn't want Madhu's issue to fray their relationship. It was, after all, a long time that Rahul was drawn to someone, emotionally and mentally, with whom he had found a solid connect. It was his insecurity of losing the perfect balance that he had created with the one he loved and desired and the one who was just a social responsibility.

Simran would often introspect, compare herself to Radha and speak aloud her thoughts to Rahul. She and Rahul had started off their relationship impetuously and now were deeply entrenched. Her confusion and complicated life now invaded on her peace of mind, her conscience rejecting her current lifestyle. She knew she was being unwise, but pulling herself away seemed impossible. She kept adjusting to Rahul's needs and wants. She wasn't prepared to leave him. She was compromising for a man, who could never be hers, just to adjust to their unique circumstances.

Another year into their relationship, Rahul had also taught Simran to recognise him as a person. He became possessive and jealous and did not encourage her to socialise on her own. He didn't know how to handle her independence.

He began to object to her tennis matches at the local club. She could not understand why he would discourage her, given his social milieu, till one day when he confronted her about her tennis matches with male partners.

'How does it matter who I am playing with? Since when did gender matter while playing a sport. And just to let you know, there are ladies as well who I play against,' Simran asked Rahul.

'Why don't you come to the club as my guest and play with us sometimes,' she added.

'I don't have the time,' he replied with a straight face.

'You have to make the time, Rahul. I'm also very busy and tired after long hours at work but still make it a point to play on weekends. Playing is so healthy,' she said, trying her best to encourage him.

'How can we be seen together? You know I have restrictions. Besides, I don't know how to play and nor am I inclined. I prefer snooker.'

'Well, it's asinine to focus on the gender while playing a sport, don't you think,' she said irritably.

'I don't like it and you should respect my feelings.'

A wave of futile rage swept over her. 'I respect your feelings, but I insist you come and watch sometimes and have tea with us after the game. No one knows you at my club, so it should be fine.'

He agreed to accompany her one afternoon, but his nervousness at being recognised and lack of interest were apparent. He kept pacing up and down impatiently waiting for the game to finish. He was curt with her friends and his eagerness to leave immediately after the game embarrassed Simran.

'It's protocol to sit after the game for some time and have tea or some drink, exchange pleasantries and then leave. We were rather rude walking off like this,' she could not help but show her annoyance.

'I don't like you hanging around with those guys and girls. Is that clear?' He could not curtail his possessiveness or his authoritative attitude.

There was no point arguing with someone who was not willing to reason. Simran disliked his sarcasm every time she went to the club. He made it a point to spoil her mood and make her feel guilty.

She knew he was being unfair and she was not going to let his insular attitude impair her confidence. Increasingly, Simran felt more like a doormat. She loved Rahul, but this side of him was just not acceptable. Madhu's growing issues did compel Simran to question herself but was she prepared to just walk out on Rahul?

Simran humoured him in the beginning, and sometimes gave in to his demands of dressing in a particular way or not going out to a particular place, and so on. Initially amused at his demands, she gradually grew uncomfortable when she had to rush back home after her games. Rahul had raised a huge hue and cry over her staying back for coffee or for a friendly chit chat after a game. His irrational behaviour encouraged her to keep things from him. She truly loathed lying to him but his demands were sometimes outright illogical. At times, she chose not to inform him when she stepped out with some of her acquaintances, or with Madhu; deliberately doing so in the morning hours of the weekend, when Rahul would wake up late. She hated these subterfuges but then she needed that freedom. This was the time when she caught up with her friends. Simran had had a liberal upbringing and these constraints made her feel claustrophobic. The fear of losing Rahul made her weak and vulnerable; forcing her to indulge him every time.

However, without realising, this was the beginning of the resentment that began to build up within Simran. Little did she realise that her sandcastle of love was about to be washed away and the brutal reality would make it difficult for her to even recognise the man she loved.

There was another incident that added to her bitterness.

She had had a bad attack of viral and didn't have the number of a doctor who would agree to a home visit; she was too weak to drive to a clinic. Although Ruby had insisted on driving her down to a doctor, Simran did not want to inconvenience Ruby, as her friend had prior plans with Anil. She turned to Rahul for help.

He was the closest person to her in Delhi and turning to him was something she just took for granted. She may not have been his legally wedded wife but she was a huge part of his life, and standing by each other, in crisis, was something Simran expected. If she was willing to stand by him and share his day-to-day problem about work, children or his on-going disharmony with Sonia, the least he could do was give her the support when she was terribly ill. She had heard that their family physician came over to check on the children and his parents. So she requested him for the doctor's number.

'It's not a good idea. I am sure we can find another doctor in the neighbourhood.'

Simran was shocked at this reply. She noticed he was being guarded.

'Why another doctor, Rahul? You already know one,' Simran asked.

'I would prefer not to involve my family doctor. Let's arrange someone else,' he said politely, but she could read the stubbornness in his voice.

'But why go hunting for someone else, when you already know a doctor?' Simran was in no mood to indulge him now.

'I don't want a common doctor,' he said, looking away. 'How will the doctor know? I could just be a stranger calling. You are being unreasonable, Rahul,' she said.

'Don't insist on this, Simran,' he said firmly.

Simran was irritated at this unnecessary cautiousness. As she lay in bed, seething, she thought about *why she had chosen this path for herself. Was she willing to be relegated as a* dark secret *of his life? Wasn't love meant to be celebrated?*

That evening when Rahul left her place, after tending to her for a couple of hours–checking her temperature, making sure she had food within hand's reach and if she was comfortably tucked in bed–Simran noticed that she did not feel the same warmth at his presence and the same longing when she heard the front door shut after him. She felt disheartened that he could not put aside his need to protect himself even though she needed a doctor's attention.

Eventually, it was Ruby who came to her rescue and arranged for a doctor. Simran, by then, was so indisposed she could barely lift her head from the pillow or put a morsel in her mouth. Rahul was missing from her bedside; he had to go to Agra for some important business meetings. Simran had dismissed his urgency to get to Agra as another of his tactics to avoid an unpleasant situation.

The doctor insisted on an injection to speed up recovery.

She did not feel the need to update Rahul on her health after the doctor left–for the first time, in over four years, she felt detached from him. It would have been unthinkable before, but suddenly she just wanted to be left alone.

But he called to enquire about her health. She was happy to hear his voice, leaving her grievances aside, but was taken aback by his question, 'Where did you take the injection?'

'What kind of a stupid question is that? On my arms, obviously,' Simran responded irritably.

Rahul realised that it would be better to make light of the situation, rather than be sarcastic. After all, he wasn't there when he was needed the most. Better sense prevailed and he laughed and said, 'I'm jealous; can't see anyone else touching you, my love. Be it the doctor.'

But Simran got the drift of where the conversation was headed. She said, firmly, 'The injection was absolutely necessary for my recovery.'

'Of course,' came the reply.

There was silence at the other end of the line.

Simran realised that his possessiveness was crossing absurd levels. She was shaking with anger; her ill health only added to her indignation.

She clenched the cell phone, when she actually wanted to fling it across the room and end this conversation. He had been unsympathetic to go away on his business trip without a thought of how she would cope with her illness all alone... Now, why was he feigning concern? She told herself not to be a wimp and allow this man to dictate her life in this illogical way.

'Rahul, I want to be left alone now,' Simran said after a while.

There was a five-second silence on the other end.

'You are overreacting, relax...' Rahul said finally.

By then Simran had just disconnected the call.

She drifted off to sleep soon afterwards, unable to shake off the unpleasantness of the conversation with Rahul.

The next morning was a better one. The medication had worked. She was in better spirits so she took her cup of tea to the balcony. It was quite early in the morning and she watched people going about their activities; children waiting for their school bus, vendors pushing their carts into the lanes hoping for early morning business, sweepers with their brooms cleaning the streets. She, in particular, noticed the happy and calm faces of the people; even the sweeper who was now in front of her gate looked content with himself. Simran wondered when she had last felt so calm and composed.

Her current differences with Rahul only added to the unpleasantness within her, she acknowledged. She attributed this to the fact they had been together for over four years now and had certainly crossed their so-called *honeymoon period.* The differences between them arose now primarily because of their expectations from each other which they could not fulfil; *was it justified to have expected Rahul cancel his business trip to be with her during her illness? And did he really expect her to be at his beck and call; waiting for him all the time?*

Rahul returned from his Agra trip and came to see her after a week. By then Simran had decided that she would not bring up the issue of her illness. She was happy to see him but noticed that he was somewhat edgy and quiet and asked him if all was well.

Sonia had become suspicious that there was another woman in his life.

Simran took the news calmly, and asked, 'Ok. What brought this on?'

'Ok? Simran, it is not ok... How can you even suggest that this is ok?' Rahul snapped.

Irritably, Simran asked him again, 'What brought this on, Rahul?'

He finally related, verbatim, what had happened immediately on his return from Agra.

'Are you having an affair, Rahul?' Sonia asked him abruptly when they had retired to their room after dinner.

'What makes you ask me such an absurd question?' Rahul responded with caution.

Sonia snapped, 'Why do you avoid spending time with me? You lock yourself up in your office room on the terrace. I do not even know what time you come to bed.'

'I have a lot of work Sonia. And I also want to catch up on some reading. What is your problem? Don't you realise how inundated with work I am?' Rahul retaliated. But he could sense acrimony brewing.

'You can read in the bedroom. I have noticed you spend more time out of the bedroom than in it,' Sonia pointed out.

Rahul knew she was going to get into a long-drawn argument and he was adamant not to battle with words.

'That is not true!' he said, avoiding eye contact.

'I have noticed that you avoid spending time with me alone in the bedroom,' Sonia observed.

'Rubbish! Stop your imagination from working overtime.'

'Are you purposely avoiding me at night?' Sonia asked directly.

'Why should I avoid you? Chill, I have a long day tomorrow, let's go to sleep.'

'It's been a while since we were intimate, what's wrong?' Sonia asked calmly; she was not going to let go.

Rahul switched off the bedside lamp to end this inquisition. Sonia reached out to him but he ignored her.

'Can we work out something for ourselves? I know something is amiss between us and let's rectify it...for our kids...for the family. We should try,' Sonia said in a restrained tone.

She switched on her bedside lamp and sat up, 'Rahul! Are you staying away from me because you have another woman in your life?'

It was all that was needed for Rahul to lose his patience. 'Please stop this nonsense. I have told you many times to keep yourself busy. I am stressed, tired and have meetings tomorrow. Can I please sleep?' he shouted.

Sonia jumped out of bed and switched on the bedroom lights.

'No, I want to talk now. Are you having an affair?'

'What's wrong with you? I don't have time to have an affair. Can't you see that I am loaded with work? Can I please get some sleep?'

'Rahul, I am no fool. Who is it? I am going to get to the bottom of this,' she threatened.

He did not respond to this, and instead, just turned his back to her, pretending to have been overcome by sleep. He hoped that she would calm down by the next morning and the situation would blow over. She carried on a monologue for a while and then fell silent.

But sleep eluded Rahul. He was however afraid to even toss and turn; Sonia might start again! He wondered at his life with Sonia. When had the equations altered between them? He had loved Sonia and found her extremely desirable. What brought about this disenchantment? Her fragrance didn't do anything for him now and why had she cut her long flowing hair? Of course it was not just the hair and the physical attraction; they had nothing in common. Their lives had just steered into opposite directions! When he finally fell off to sleep, his last thought was a silent prayer that Sonia did not begin again the next morning.

Rahul woke up to a brooding Sonia.

He now told Simran that things had drastically changed since then; Sonia's suspicion kicked in new demands and she frequently dropped by at the office in the evenings when he was wrapping up work so he was forced to accompany her home. She ensured he was invited for family lunches which he would not refuse. And on most evenings when she did not land up at the office, she called to let him know that friends or relatives had dropped over; so he would have to rush back home. This blocked Simran and Rahul's 11 pm chats, something he looked forward to.

Even on that day, when he had slipped out early from office to get to Simran's place, he was sure that he was being followed; that Sonia was spying on him. So he had deliberately parked his car far away from her house and slipped into an auto rickshaw to get here.

Simran's first reaction was that of amusement; she adored Rahul for his tricks to avoid his so-called pursuer. *But was Sonia really having him followed,* she wondered.

Rahul added, 'Now she makes sure Nalini, our daughter, is there in the office. The poor girl wants to become an interior designer and has no interest in my line of work.'

'Rahul, you have to sort this out yourself,' Simran couldn't think of solutions. She then added, 'I get very little time with you...chatting in the night is the least you can do.'

'There isn't much I can do; she has friends drop in every other day... I have to be a good host.'

'Whatever! I need your time too.'

Rahul stated how he had to even humour her demands for physical intimacy and attention.

Simran felt as if she had been punched right in the face.

Hadn't he given her the impression that there was no love between Sonia and him for years? How could he even tell her now that he was playing the perfect husband in every way just to get her off his back? What was the desperation in not wanting to rock the boat?

As the questions flooded Simran's mind, she came face to face with an important aspect of Rahul's character; that he was willing to do just about anything to ensure that nothing disturbed the status quo of his life. Simran could understand his concern for the children but why did it have to so desperately stretch to Sonia.

As Rahul continued to groan about how he was beginning to feel claustrophobic with Sonia's demands for attention, Simran had to fight back the desire to snap back at him or simply ask him to admit to Sonia's allegations. That way they would all be set free from their respective distress.

Although Rahul stayed with her for a couple of hours, Simran could sense that he was preoccupied. She could not empathise with his predicament and when Rahul finally left she was confused at her own feeling. It wasn't as painful to see him go.

The situation at home began to affect Rahul's peace of mind. Simran missed that charming man who had literally swept her off her feet with his wit and earnestness; here was this man who was grouchy and preferred to sit and brood over his cup of coffee. The conversations between them now lacked vitality and Simran wondered *why he bothered to come over if he was in no mood to talk.*

She had become so accustomed to his pampering that this sudden change in behaviour was disconcerting.

~

Holi was around the corner. Though Simran did not play with colours, she wanted to spend the festival with Rahul; she had never encroached on his *festival time for family policy* but now she needed to be with him for the assurance that she too was important to him. He had now put her self-respect and dignity at stake.

But it was easier said than done. Rahul's extended family usually came over and it was a ritual to play Holi in the sprawling garden of his house. It was usually a huge gathering; most of his relatives were in Delhi; only his sister and her children would come over from Mumbai.

It was totally a family affair and the kids in particular were extremely enthusiastic. They often invited their own group of friends and the combination of three generations making merry together made it a fun occasion. Preparations began days in advance and Rahul had begun to relate every miniscule detail to Simran. He enjoyed playing host, especially as festival times meant a lot to his mother.

Simran knew that such occasions were strictly meant for family. *There was no place for her there. Rahul would never spend Holi with her; she had to be content with whatever little time he could spare for her. She was a covert aspect of his life and he could never bring her face to face with his family and friends.* These thoughts made her sad and depressed and persisted even though she tried to push them away. She could not voice her desire to Rahul and after her customary call to Karishma and her parents on the day of Holi, she sat quietly at home, listening to the sound of the revelry outside. Usually, she was glad to be indoors when the world outside gave in to their playful side irrespective of their age and gender, but this Holi, she was itching to go outside and be part of the merriment, but, with Rahul. She wished so just for the sheer joy of sharing Rahul's happiness.

Madhu and Ruby knew that she was not fond of playing Holi so they chose not to disturb her, apart from the standard Holi text messages. Simran wished that Ruby, with her usual wilfulness had dragged her out to some Holi party somewhere.

Eventually, to snap out of her current mood, she ventured out for a drive alone; she wasn't going to feel sorry for herself. Cars zipped past her, some even bombarding her car with balloons and shouting 'Holi *hai.*' She remembered as a child she would play with her neighbours all day till her mother scolded her to come home. The high point of school the next day was to see the tinge of green, red, purple and other colours on the faces of her classmates; a testimony to how enthusiastically they had enjoyed the festival. She remembered Karishma's first Holi, the moppet had bawled when she hadn't been able to recognise her parents.

Rahul called her several times during the day to say that he missed her. Simran's face broke into a smile every time his name flashed on the cell phone display; maybe he could sense that she was lonely. This must surely augur well for their relationship; it showed that despite their recent differences, they were still tuned in to each other's moods.

Rahul felt guilty that Simran was spending this festival day alone but circumstances at home were demanding.

I'll work it out, Rahul told himself. *But moving away from Simran is not possible.*

CHAPTER 10

With Ruby on her way to matrimony and Madhu's marriage breaking up, Simran had become more aware of the deception she had been living for the past couple of years. She began questioning herself, *where her relationship with Rahul was heading? Could she expect a lifelong commitment from him?* But *why expect* a lifelong commitment? After her divorce, she did not want to remarry. Why then, was she expecting legal privileges akin to those of a spouse? Why put the blame squarely on Rahul? Simran was an equal player in this relationship.

While Simran was unsure, and confused, she acknowledged that she was tired of being the afterthought; the one always waiting in the wings for his attention. Somehow, she knew that it was because of her own actions that he had become the centre of her existence. Simran wondered how she had let that happen. She chided herself for putting aside all her expectations just to ensure that things always stayed amicable between them. Even when she felt bereft at the thought of spending festivals alone, Simran had never demanded that he should go out of his way to be with her. However, now the borrowed hour every evening was not enough. The holidays during his official trips, a few times in the year, did not fill the void and the alienation from his social life made her feel belittled. Above that, Sonia's suspicions did not make their trysts any easier. She wanted to fortify her marriage and not abdicate her domain to the possibility of another woman in Rahul's life.

They could not socialise and could not be seen in public; therefore, almost all the times they met, it had to be at her flat. Initially, Simran revelled in the privacy; it was their love-nest. But now she was finding this constraint claustrophobic.

Simran wanted to change the current status quo. But how could she do this without getting into a confrontation with Rahul. After pondering over this for days at end, she finally came to a decision. She would ask Rahul to spend this year's Diwali with her.

While Rahul projected a nonchalant attitude about the way their relationship was drifting, Simran was growing weary of the lonely life she was expected to lead.

The previous years had been different. Those were the days when they longed to be with each other all the time; the novelty of their situation added the requisite thrill.

But now, there had even been five to 10-minute meetings, several times during the day, in the days leading up to the festival, because he was not bound to be in the office the whole day. Simran acknowledged to herself that this would actually be a test for Rahul to prove his commitment to her during Diwali which was a busy time for him. This year too he had been going about the city distributing gifts to family and friends. For a month before the festival he had only been making fleeting visits to her place; dropping by for 15-20 minutes when he was in the vicinity. She had not made a fuss over this. She was waiting for the right time.

The day before Diwali Simran called Rahul.

'Rahul, I would like to spend this Diwali with you. Will you come early, so that we can do the *pooja* together?'

There was a stunned silence at the other end.

'What time can I expect you?' Simran coaxed.

'You want me to come over to your place for Diwali?' he asked incredulously.

Something in his tone made Simran sit up straight.

'What is so strange about that?' Her voice was cold.

'Simran, I cannot do that. What will I tell my family here?' He sounded almost desperate. 'And Sonia? How will I explain things to her? You know we cannot afford to make her any more suspicious.'

'You can't be serious,' Simran cut him.

'Please understand, what excuses would I make for not being at home for Diwali?' Rahul pleaded.

'That's not my problem. You say what you have to Rahul and don't ruin my Diwali,' Simran said curtly, putting up a brave front. But she admitted the sad truth that Rahul had not come up to her mark.

'Why are you being difficult? I will make it up to you and spend a full day with you next week,' he offered.

'Oh really! You must be crazy to suggest that I spend Diwali on my own. You know Karishma and my parents have gone for a holiday to Ooty. You are the one who discouraged me from going with them.'

'Simran, please try to understand. I don't want a scene at home with Sonia, with my parents getting involved. You know that she is suspicious. My relatives will be here and I don't want a disgruntled woman on my hands,' Rahul tried to convince Simran.

By now Simran could sense her resentment against Rahul rising like bile inside her throat. But she was not going to let him have his way this time. She had always prided herself for being a strong woman.

'Let's at least do *pooja* together,' Simran said finally, knowing that he would have to overstretch his imagination to even ensure that on the day of Diwali. He agreed to come over. Or maybe he did not want to escalate the issue with her.

Disconnecting the call she told herself that she had once again settled for whatever little he could give her. *Am I really any different from the women who take years of neglect and callousness just for a scrap of attention?*

Simran was cold and distant when Rahul came over on the evening of Diwali for the *pooja.* The sight of him irked her. She hastened through the *pooja*, increasingly getting annoyed with each passing minute. She knew that she was forcing him to stretch his time to accommodate her. And she still could not sense that he empathised with her situation. He was here because she had forced him. Everything appeared fake—even his smiling face was an eye sore.

'You can go back to Sonia now,' she said curtly as they finished the *pooja*.

'Simran, you know I would rather...' Rahul started but she interrupted him asking him to go back home before his family started calling and he ran out of excuses to mollify them.

The moment he left she called Ruby and requested if she could join Anil and her for the Diwali celebrations. Madhu and the girls also joined them. It was a sombre Diwali. She began to question the last few years she had given to him, making him the epicentre of her life.

Simran's answering machine was jammed with messages from Rahul when she returned from Ruby's place; it did nothing to put her mind to rest. He had also sent umpteen text messages, apologising for not being with her for Diwali and promising to spend more time with her henceforth. Simran had not bothered to respond.

She got into bed but could not fall asleep. Episodes from the last couple of years flashed though her mind; she admitted to herself that she had indeed been happy with Rahul and had treasured the moments with him. He had taken her around the world and showered gifts and at times his tenderness had almost moved her to tears. But he did not make her happy anymore! Or at least the terms and conditions of their relationship did not make her happy anymore. She had reconciled herself to being the *outsider* in his life; somebody who would get his attention but with its own constraints. But that did not satisfy her anymore!

She had accepted that he would not be comfortable in publicly acknowledging her as an integral part of his life; she had to be content with being with him only within the confines of her apartment and during their handful of foreign trips through the year.

But she did not want to live this clandestine life anymore. She had not told her parents about Rahul and he too had expressed no desire to get acquainted with her family. *If she was so important for him shouldn't he have accepted that he had a bigger role in her life; to at least try to develop some kind of an association with her family? She had accepted that their relationship had certain limitations but now that Karishma was a teenager, well entrenched into her adolescent years, and was growing up, didn't she have a parental responsibility towards the kind of future she could offer her? Was she really expecting to keep her relationship with Rahul under wraps forever?*

For some reason, even the lies that he told his family bothered her now, for they reflected the extent to which he was willing to go to have things his way. Simran remembered how Sonia and the children were in Mumbai one New Year. Rahul had to be with them but managed to stave it off at the last minute and remained in Delhi. His family must have been upset by his absence on New Year's Day; especially the kids. For Simran however it had been a boon; the coolest New Year gift she had ever received.

But now she was besieged by indignation and guilt!

She tossed and turned in bed as these questions flooded her mind. Finally, she got out of bed to stand by the window; taking in the dark stillness outside which seemed to reflect the bleakness within her. There was a power cut as she knew from the slow droning of the fan in her room; the sound always alerted her that power was now running though the battery-operated inverter. For a few minutes the droning filled her thoughts. And then suddenly, the darkness outside was washed with light as the street lights came on with the return of electricity.

The brightness seemed to trigger something inside her.

She knew what she had to do...

CHAPTER 11

'Where the hell were you last night? I left so many messages? Why didn't you call back?' Rahul almost shouted over the phone.

How dare he be so demanding, after neglecting me, Simran thought. She casually looked at the clock on the wall. It was after 11 in the morning. She had slept in late.

'Didn't want to be alone so I went off with friends,' she replied.

'You should have told me,' was his berating tone, 'I have been worried sick about you.'

Simran wanted to tell him to get lost. But she actually said, 'I spent the evening with Ruby and Anil... What time are you coming across?'

'I will be there in the evening,' he said, realising the mood she was in and perhaps deciding that there was no point agitating her further. 'I had kept a few gifts aside so I would be able to step out of the house.'

That evening, Rahul seemed to correctly sense the atmosphere as she opened the door to let him in; the usual smile was missing and the bad mood hit him like a strong gust of warm air that had nothing to do with the heater in the sitting area. It was the end of November and the evenings were now unusually cold; heralding a really cold December and January.

He stood there at the entrance with a gift for her. *The appropriate place for his gift is on the street outside,* Simran thought.

He closed the door behind him shutting out the cold and hugged her tightly. Simran could sense her knees go weak and she clung to him for a couple of minutes with a deep sense of yearning. Some of her fears and insecurities melted in the warmth of his arms. She quickly got a grip on herself—this time she was not going to repeat her blunder and be a silly woman, content with his reassurances, pampering and coaxing.

She wanted both of them to come up with answers.

He sat on the sofa and she perched on its arm silently, her exuberance missing, but wanting to stay as close to him as possible, watching every little reaction on his face, or every little twitch of his body. He perhaps sensed that there was something on her mind and that she was restless inside.

'What's the matter?'

Come straight to the point, Simran cautiously told herself... she wanted a substantial conclusion not a squabble.

'I was very upset last evening. I got to spend just half an hour with you on Diwali,' said Simran. 'Have you started taking me for granted now?'

She had chosen her words carefully, with the right mix of hurt and anger.

He stiffened and responded irritably, 'Why are you making such a big deal about this? You know I am married and that I am answerable to someone. I don't want my wife making my life miserable. You knew it, didn't you... from the very start.'

Simran smirked! Predictable reaction!

'If your family is so important to you, then who am I? If I mean nothing to you after so many years, then why are you with me? You have no business sitting in my house, on my sofa, with me in your arms and declaring that you cannot give me enough time because you are married.'

She paused to catch her breath; keeping calm was a mammoth task. Rahul was taken aback; he hadn't expected such an explosive response.

'Simran, you mean the world to me; I don't want to let you go. I am always there for you. You are the true love of my life and Sonia is just a responsibility. Why can't you understand that and let things be? Please be sensible, Sonia is the link to the rest of my family. If this link breaks, everyone will scatter,' he said.

'So you are using Sonia to keep the family together and me for whatever else,' Simran was now fuming.

Simran pointed out that she wasn't asking him to shirk his responsibilities towards his family but he had to think about her needs too. She paused, took a deep breath and asked, 'What if I ask you to tell Sonia about me?'

She didn't blink, looked him straight in the eye, so he would not be able to look away.

He looked completely stunned.

'How did that come about? We both knew the complexities of this relationship when we decided to be together. How can you ask me to tell her now? It is not so easy. What's got into you these days, why are you so demanding?' he retorted.

Simran was prepared with an answer.

'You have your family but you expect me to isolate myself from the world. I am sick of being left out of everything. You impose so many do's and don'ts on my life.'

By now Simran's voice had gone up a few notches higher, 'I keep waiting for you to come over, putting my entire life on hold. Besides, I am fed up of all the lies and deceit.'

Simran felt relieved giving voice to the thoughts that had been troubling her.

After a pause, she continued, 'Let me make it easy for you. You tell Sonia about us. Tell her that you are not happy with her. After knowing everything, let her make her choice.'

Rahul jumped to his feet. The two now stood facing each other and in the silence that followed, Simran saw the movement of his Adam's apple as he swallowed repeatedly to find the right words.

Finally he spoke...

'It's not just about Sonia. It's about my parents and kids. Do you want things to come out in the open? It will blow up and we all will go deaf with the noise the *coming out in the open* will create. You and I have a precious thing going. Please don't complicate our lives.'

But Simran was determined not to be pushed into the sidelines again.

'Rahul, we are not living in the dark ages anymore. Kids do understand if their parents want to get separated. Karishma was very mature when she learnt that her father and I did not want to stay together anymore...and your kids are much older. So please do not make them the excuse for not telling Sonia,' Simran responded.

'And what do I tell them? That their father now has another woman in his life that he wants to bed and wed?' Rahul said, sarcastically.

Simran flinched at his words.

'Rahul, whether your children come to respect me or not, would depend on you; the way you express how important I am in your life,' she responded, trying hard to rein in her rising temper.

'How can you do this Simran when I think about you all the time and love you? What's the point of this argument? Let's sort this out like mature people. This is something new you have started. Who's egging you on? I'm sure it's your friend Madhu; I knew she would do this. I told you not to meet her?' he challenged.

'Cut this out Rahul! I have not told anybody about us; not even Ruby and Madhu. But you have to prove that you love me and that you are concerned about my well-being and happiness. You have some responsibility towards me too.'

'Come on darling, you know what you mean to me; there can't be an iota of doubt in your mind. Why make a big deal because I couldn't spend Diwali with you; it's like any other normal day.'

'Stop this nonsense please. Every occasion is a big deal, so please don't try and derail me.'

'I promise I will make it up to you. Let's plan a trip next month and spend some quality time together,' he coaxed.

But Simran was adamant. 'I don't want to go on a holiday. I want you to do this for us–tell Sonia.'

'This is not the way to handle things, Simran. It will cause a lot of disturbance. Think about my parents,' Rahul implored.

'It's your call, Rahul, I have taken mine. Your parents will understand if you try.'

'You mean the world to me. You are the love of my life and Sonia is just a responsibility, why can't you believe that and let things be...,' Rahul repeated himself, now looking nervous. 'Let us go away on a short holiday. I know you want us to spend time together.'

'You don't get it, do you, Rahul? I have made up my mind. It's time you made some definite decisions,' Simran said firmly. 'You tell Sonia about us so that there is no need for us to see each other surreptitiously anymore. I am not ashamed to have fallen in love with you, but now I want our relationship to get the dignity it deserves.'

'Well. You get all my love, what more do you want?'

Simran wasn't amused and wanted to wipe off the smugness from his face.

'Stop this charade, Rahul! I can't deal with this anymore. It hurts that I have to keep turning to my friends for company or rot alone at home when I have you in my life,' she said, choking back a sob.

She hated herself at this moment for not being able to keep a check on her emotions.

Rahul was quick to perceive the change. He moved forward and put his arm around her.

'I think about you all the time and love you. What you are asking for is not so easy!'

Rahul knew how one impulsive step, guided purely by emotions, could land him into deep trouble. He had to talk Simran out of this crazy idea, he told himself now. He needed time to think things through. He wondered if Madhu's problems were influencing Simran. *What had suddenly got into her?*

'I just can't live this secretive life anymore. You have to understand where I am coming from,' Simran said, having decided to hold her ground.

Rahul now looked nervous. 'You have to be sensible... you...'

'It's your call Rahul.'

'This...this...this is too drastic,' Rahul stuttered.

To say 'it's over' or 'we are finished' would have been like plunging a dagger into my heart, Simran thought as she stared at him.

'I repeat, Rahul. You have to prove how important I am in your life.' Simran asserted.

Sensing that this was an ultimatum, Rahul, without saying a word, just walked out of the front door.

Later, as she lay in bed, drained of all energy and emotion, she thought back on the conversation. *Why did Rahul keep insisting that they go away together on a holiday? Were the holidays just an emotional bribe to prevent her from getting cantankerous?* Maybe, they were exactly that. He showered her with so much attention during these trips that on their return she always felt guilty about demanding anything more from him–including his time.

Was Rahul really this calculative? Was she in a relationship with a completely wrong person?

Was she still in a relationship? she wondered.

Rahul had walked out of her house; what was on his mind?

CHAPTER 12

Simran was really restless after Rahul left. *What was her future with Rahul,* she asked herself repeatedly. Taking her troubles to her friends would mean opening herself to questions and perhaps even criticism. So she went to the chemist, bought some sleeping pills, popped in two and putting her phone off the hook crashed out in bed. All she wanted was to blank out and rest. The dreaded sleeping pill was the new addition to her life.

In spite of the sleeping pills, she slept restlessly that night and automatically reached for the phone first thing in the morning. There was no message from Rahul. She remembered the angst of the previous evening and the way Rahul had left without any conclusive decision. Should she call him or just wait patiently? Was he going to tell Sonia about them or would he just dismiss her request? She had to wait and see how he chose to deal with the situation. She had to give him that space.

If Rahul told his family about her, she had the moral responsibility to tell her parents too. They had been disappointed with her decision about living in Delhi after her divorce; they had tried convincing her time and again, to move to Chennai, but she preferred her independence. She was determined to move forward and returning home was not an option.

Just then the phone rang. It was her mother. Perfect! Her mother was too perceptive. She would immediately detect any kind of anxiety, if any, in her voice.

'Mom, can I call you later?' Simran said, attempting to cut short the conversation.

She knew if she didn't take the call, this early in the morning, her mother would get worried.

'Are you unwell?... Has something happened?' There was panic in her mother's voice.

'Take it easy mom. I just woke up. I will speak to you in a while.'

'Are you sure that is the reason? Simran, I am really worried about you, why didn't you call yesterday. Is there something I should know?' her mother insisted.

'Please stop mom... I have just woken up and now I am getting a headache. I will call back after I have had some tea and breakfast. I am hungry. I didn't have my dinner.'

'No dinner! Are you unwell? Is everything ok?'

'Oh god! Don't get started again. I said I will call later,' Simran said in exasperation, wishing she had left the phone ringing.

She was not ready to tell all to her mother now; needed time to sort out her thoughts. Her mother finally disconnected when Simran told her that she would call back in exactly an hour's time.

Her thoughts went back to Rahul. She realised that they had arrived at the crossroads of their relationship. *If push came to shove,* she asked herself, *would she be able to relinquish her attachment?* She was not sure; torn as she was between her heart and her head. *Which would prove stronger? But could she face being alone again?* Loneliness could play havoc with self-esteem and push thoughts in destructive directions.

For the rest of the day Simran went about her house like an automaton; cleaning here and dusting there, but made sure her cell phone was within hand's reach. She kept checking for messages from Rahul. But there were none. He had simply gone incommunicado! She quelled the panic that threatened to overwhelm her at the possibility that Rahul might have just decided to end their relationship.

Get a grip on yourself Simran, she admonished herself, *Rahul and you are not college-going kids who fall out at the first sign of trouble.*

But she had to acknowledge the possibility that Rahul might step back as he had now been pushed against the wall.`

The next morning, after a sleepless night wracked by roller-coaster emotions, Simran felt drained. The phone rang and she grabbed it.

It was Rahul.

'Hi beautiful, you awake? Had your morning cup of tea? Guess what, I have decided to take the day off and spend the entire day with you. In fact, I was wondering if you would like to go to Agra this weekend. I could always take off on the pretext of work,' he finished breathlessly, almost as though this was a well-rehearsed speech.

Simran listened in disbelief. How could he carry on the charade and want to go off on a trip when there were unresolved issues between them?

Maybe she needed to remind him again.

She asked him whether he had given a serious thought to what they had discussed.

'Why are you not relenting? It seems you have made up your mind to just go on and on about this? Why are you hell-bent on making things unpleasant between us?' Rahul snapped back.

Simran wanted to tell him to be a man and take the bull by its horns... instead she took deep breaths, trying to calm herself down.

With no response from her end, he asked, 'What do you want me to do?'

'You know what needs to be done. I am not happy with the way things are going. How long can we sustain a relationship like this?' Simran responded, almost willing him to understand.

'Are you saying that you are not happy with me?'

'Rahul, you are misunderstanding me completely,' she said.

'But it's coming across like that...'

'You have to understand how I feel; that I am not really a part of your life and lonely. We are in a relationship; we need to share a life. Rahul, you need to ask yourself some serious questions. Besides, do you feel happy with all the lies you have to keep telling Sonia?'

'The kids and my parents will suffer if I tell Sonia anything,' Rahul repeated his arguments from two days ago.

'Well, in that case we have to re-evaluate our lives with each other. I need to respect myself. You have to play fair.'

'Ok...ok...can you drop it now? Let me think about it. Are we meeting this evening? Or will that make you unhappy again?'

Rahul admitted to himself that his bond with Simran was extraordinary but she was really pushing him towards the impossible now! *Why was she being so stubborn?* He had a cantankerous wife back home; he certainly did not need a nagging girlfriend. The hours seemed to crawl but evening eventually did arrive and so did Rahul. He entered and held her tight in his arms and whispered in her ear, 'Have it your way. I will tell Sonia. But please cut me some slack. I can't handle being badgered at both ends.'

Simran was baffled; did she hear him right? It couldn't be that simple. But his words were like a balm to her heart. She had not imagined such a smooth run... In fact, she was prepared for another round of bitter arguments.

Rahul continued, 'I'll find an appropriate time and tell her. She is already suspicious and it would be better if she hears it from me. She's a good woman and it is not her fault that I am not in love with her. My main concern is the effect on my children. I want to spare them the trauma.'

Simran was delirious with joy, but one part of her mind could not help being suspicious. *Did he really mean it?* After all, it was not going to be easy for the family. She however pushed these thoughts aside and clung to him, as if she would never let him go. Tears of happiness were streaming down her face.

Later, after Rahul had left, Simran found herself contemplating the future. *How would Sonia take the news? Would she still choose to live with Rahul? Would she choose to confront her? How would Rahul's family take the news? And if Sonia decided to get a legal separation from Rahul, would he now contemplate marriage with her?*

Simran admitted to herself that she did not have much faith in the institution of marriage. She was financially secure and did not have to depend on anybody; it was liberating. She had managed to open her own small export factory which was running successfully. She was supplying handbags to a niche market in Malaysia. The stock market had given her decent dividends and she had bought a small flat which she had rented out.

With these questions came the anxiety over how the society at large would react to her. Would she be seen as the *home-breaker*? But there was no emotional connect between Rahul and Sonia before she entered the picture. *Would she be able to make that fact known? More importantly, did she care about how the world perceived her?* Torn between the need to be accepted and defiant about the existing mores of a society that she knew would be too quick to judge her and her motives, Simran decided to just wait and bide time till things started moving in any particular direction.

CHAPTER 13

Madhu's life, in the meanwhile, had hit rock bottom. Raghav was adamant to march on. He felt that Madhu was using the kids as a tool for her negotiations. She was forced to talk to him through her lawyer, as she could find no other solution; Raghav was rigid and disagreed with Madhu's terms of settlement. He did not want to dispense with the alimony amount that Madhu was demanding and her health had started deteriorating because of the stress.

One evening, Madhu called over Simran and Ruby to her place. Simran and Ruby rushed over as she had sounded really upset. 'Raghav is conniving with the landlord to throw me out,' these were Madhu's first words as her friends entered the house. 'He wants to push me against the wall so that I settle for whatever little he agrees to give me.'

'How do you know all this?' Ruby's face registered immediate concern.

'My landlord came over and asked me to vacate the place. Raghav hasn't paid the rent and has told him that he will be giving up his tenancy,' Madhu responded, stoic.

'He wants me out of his life as soon as possible,' Madhu added.

'That's ok, you surely don't want him either, but he has to agree to a fair amount as settlement so that you do not have to worry about a roof over your head and education for the girls,' Simran responded, the only calm voice in front of her two agitated friends.

She put an arm around Madhu's shoulder as an assurance. 'You have to be strong through this Madhu. I know it will be difficult but you cannot go to pieces before the girls. You cannot remind them again and again that their lives have been set adrift. This is a tragedy, we all agree. But you will really not get anything out of this by cursing Raghav.'

She looked at Ruby as she said this.

'Pick up your life Madhu. And start doing what you need to and stop crying at the very mention of Raghav.'

'The feeling of not having a roof over your head is so scary...I go through sleepless nights just thinking about it. I suffer from anxiety attacks. My only saving grace is my sister,' Madhu said, unable to hold back her sobs.

'Have you spoken to your sister and brother-in-law?' Ruby asked, finally able to appreciate the drift of Simran's words.

'Yes, my brother-in-law and sister have agreed to help till I am on my feet again...'

They were trying to determine the next course of action when the doorbell rang and the postman delivered Madhu's divorce papers. She concentrated on reading the papers, unable to hold back her tears; her hands were trembling and she started perspiring.

'I did not feel so isolated even when my parents passed away. My life revolved around Raghav; he was the person I trusted the most and he has let me down... It's unimaginable...all this seems like a bad dream.'

As Simran watched Madhu consoling her daughters over their lives falling apart, she wondered how she would take it if Rahul and her relationship collapsed. She was glad that she had not brought Karishma into the picture yet. If things went completely wrong, at least she would not have to explain things to her daughter. She had done this once. Not again...never again. But then, she chided herself for the negative thoughts. Rahul was going to tell Sonia about them. Everything would fall into place after that. Simran thought of Sonia, *wouldn't she be in the same predicament as Madhu?* She pushed the thoughts away.

~

A week passed but Rahul still hadn't told Sonia–the house was full of visitors was the reason he gave. Although annoyed, Simran trusted Rahul and believed in him. He had made a commitment and he had never given her any reason to mistrust him.

But a month went by, then two...then three...and Rahul still had not spoken to Sonia. Simran began wondering why he was delaying it. Something was surely amiss! *Was he just spinning these lame excuses and hoping that the issue would die a natural death; thinking she would come around with time?* Simran was slowly losing her patience.

In the first month, after the decision was taken to open up to Sonia about their relationship, Simran and

Rahul had numerous arguments over the delay—with Simran pushing him to tell Sonia, and Rahul insisting that the timing was not appropriate. But gradually these altercations also stopped; Simran realised that it was futile getting into a confrontation with him.

She decided to rock the boat just a little; she shut her doors on him and left for Chennai to spend time with her daughter and her parents. Her mother had not been keeping well.

Rahul could not trace her and she refused to take his calls.

The day she returned, the guard informed her that Rahul had stopped by a few times. He had been sending her umpteen texts, but she had ignored all. One of the messages read, *Are you holding me to ransom?*

Perhaps I am! She told herself. He had to understand that she meant business. The landline was ringing as she entered her apartment. She knew it was Rahul and decided to take the call.

'Where the hell have you been? Why have you been ignoring me?' he shouted.

She could sense the frustration in his voice but was in no mood to listen to a barrage of angry words. So she simply hung up.

The phone rang at least 20 times after that and then in 20 minutes Rahul was at her place. He held her in his arms as though he would never let her go.

'Rahul...what... What are you doing here at this time of the day?' Simran tried to make light of the situation, but her voice choked. There was something very unnerving about seeing Rahul in tears. It showed how deeply he cared for her. She almost felt sorry that she had taken off just to spite him.

However, the issue still stood between them like a cold stone wall. In spite of her emotional reaction to him, she knew that he was the one who had to take the initiative and knock the wall down; he had to tell Sonia and show her that he really cared and if he did not want to, he had to be honest and give her the choice to choose her own path.

She kept her face as passive as possible when she asked him if he had done what she had asked him to, in her absence. Rahul avoided meeting her eyes as he told her that he had not got the opportunity.

'Are you planning to tell her? I mean if you don't want to then I would rather not force you,' Simran responded with sarcasm.

'I will tell her, Simran. Please understand that it is not so easy... My parents, my kids...our friends...' Rahul implored.

'I know about all of them...but I also know that I do not want this half-hearted commitment from you.'

'Half-hearted? Do you think I am not committed...'

'Stop this pretence please. You know what I am talking about. Let us not confuse the issue here.'

The coldness of her tone seemed to finally get to him and he promised in all earnestness that he would tell Sonia.

For some odd reason, she had a tough time accepting the sincerity in his voice. 'Call me when you have told Sonia,' Simran said, as she guided him to the front door.

There was no call from Rahul the day after...neither on the next day...nor on the following day. When he did call it was to tell her that Sonia's aunt was visiting so he had not got the opportunity to talk. She told him to not call her till he had done the needful.

For several days after this Rahul kept sending her texts asking for more time. Simran did not bother to respond to his messages and even refused to take his calls; she was just tired of his excuses. Simran's patience was growing thin and she felt detached from her circumstance. *Should I give up? I deserve to be happy. If I can move on from a broken marriage, stand on my own, then why should I be subjected to this mental agony?* There were days when she would curl up in her bed all day and cry. She was getting habituated to sleeping pills and feared that she was approaching chronic depression. There were times when she was tempted to call him and run into his arms; forget the promise! *I cannot bear to stay away from you,* she wanted to say. But she then checked herself with the thought that Rahul had to prove that she was more to him than just a shady secret. This was the least that he could do and the very least that she deserved.

CHAPTER 14

Despite the emotional roller-coaster that Simran and Madhu's respective lives were in, they had to ensure that they were happy for Ruby.

She was enthusiastic about organising her engagement party. Most of the preparations were now complete. In spite of the merriment all around, there were moments when Simran was besieged by sadness. Ruby noticed that her friend often had an anguished expression on her face.

'What's the matter Simran, you look so tormented. What's bothering you? I know I have put a lot of responsibilities on your shoulder. I hope it is not causing too much stress.'

Simran immediately put on her broadest smile, 'Nothing like that Ruby. I am just concerned about Madhu's situation. She is emotionally distraught and looks so lost all the time. She has still not been able to come to terms with her situation, however strong a front she is putting up.'

She yearned to reveal about what was going on in her life; being the strong one, Ruby could surely help Simran handle the situation better. But the timing was not correct. She was about to enter the most wonderful period of her life and she deserved to take in only happiness from her surroundings.

'It makes me wonder...if I am making the right choice. If Madhu and Raghav can split up, anything can happen...' Ruby mused, and after a pause, added, 'Let's keep Madhu busy. At least she will get her mind off her problems for a few days. Do you think you can involve her with the catering arrangements? She can do the food tasting and work out the linen, crockery and cutlery.'

'What a fantastic idea! Let her also do the flowers and decorations. I will help her, but let her take the lead,' Simran offered.

Just then they noticed Madhu walking through the garden towards them.

'Hello gorgeous! What are you wearing on my engagement and marriage? I want to see it before you wear it; you have to look ravishing,' Ruby spoke to Madhu.

'I have decided and I am picking it up the day after tomorrow... You can come along with Simran and me,' Madhu replied. 'I don't know how I will look though. My daughters have been telling me that I have started looking very pale. Sorry Ruby, it's a bad time for me.'

'Rubbish, you look beautiful. I am going to hook you up with someone really nice,' Ruby joked and went on to hug her.

'Spare me the horror,' Madhu piped up with a smile.

'There are many nice men out there... Ok Madhu, I need you to look into the catering and flower decorations with Simran. In fact, please shift into my house for a few days with the girls. There is a lot of work and I need you to be around.' Ruby was determined to give Madhu some respite from her misery, even if it was only for a few days.

'No, no, I will manage from home.'

'Think about it Madhu. It's a good idea. It would be like a mini holiday. The girls will love it,' Simran also encouraged her.

Madhu hugged Ruby with moist eyes, 'Ok, thank you, what would I do without you girls. Now you don't worry. Simran and I will manage everything.'

Ruby's engagement party was a grand success. They boogied the night away to Bollywood songs. From the latest Bollywood chartbusters to yesteryear oldies, all were being played by the DJ. Her two-carat diamond ring was stunning. The friends could not resist laughing when Anil slipped it on her finger.

'What a fancy rubber band,' Sharmila laughed.

Anil looked confused.

'She said she wouldn't mind a rubber band as her engagement ring, Anil. Love...love is all she wanted,' Sharmila explained.

'Why didn't you girls tell me earlier? I would have saved on a lot of money!' Anil said in mock indignation, before adding, 'Someone quickly get me a rubber band so that I can return the ring tomorrow.'

He pretended to put the ring back into his pocket.

Everyone burst out laughing.

Simran and Madhu watched the happy couple with a smile on their respective faces; each wishing that her life was as uncomplicated as Ruby's.

Dinner was served. Simran, Madhu and her girls sat together, exhausted. In the background, Anil and Ruby got up to dance with everyone cheering them on. Simran and Madhu looked at the couple in silence, their eyes moist...

Simran wished that had it been normal circumstances, Rahul might have joined them in the celebrations and they could be on the dance floor now, with Anil and Ruby. It would have made this day more memorable for her.

Ruby was determined that this was the perfect occasion to introduce Simran to Anil's friends. 'Simran, it's about time you meet someone nice. Anil has some friends he will introduce you to.' What could Simran say; she already had a man in her life but could not talk to them about him.

CHAPTER 15

Rahul, in the meanwhile, had been completely thrown off balance because of Simran's demand. He knew she was strong-minded and determined to have him reveal their liaison. At times, he even contemplated terminating his relationship with Simran, but life without her seemed impossible. He was angry with her for disrupting their peaceful romance. But after a lot of deliberation, he decided to come clean with Sonia.

Simran had been ignoring Rahul for a couple of weeks now. One afternoon, his number flashed and she ignored it, as usual, even though she longed to grab the receiver. Then the landline rang, which she did not bother to pick up. The answering machine came on.

'I have told Sonia. Will you pick up your damn phone?'

She froze, at a loss for words, and lunged for the receiver. Rahul sounded exhausted. 'God, it was the most harrowing night of my life!' Rahul explained, 'I managed some sleep only at five in the morning. Sonia went ballistic.'

'Well, what else did you expect? Nobody likes being rejected.'

'I tried to convince her that we had drifted apart. I appealed to her better sense of judgement that we should free ourselves of the burden of an unhappy relationship, but she just wouldn't listen to anything,' Rahul said, sounding tired.

'What exactly did she say?' Simran asked.

'I'm too tired to recall everything verbatim now,' Rahul dismissed her query, and added, 'Get lunch organised please. The lack of sleep last night has resulted in a splitting headache... This is what you wanted...so there...I've done it.'

Simran did not respond to the sarcasm... It was best to let Rahul let off steam. She was sure that Sonia was not going to reconcile to the situation easily.

What happened in the next few weeks was beyond anything Rahul and Simran had expected. Sonia went silent after Rahul broke the news at home. Sonia's friends and family insulted and maligned Simran, who faced the brunt of all the anger that came from every quarter. Simran had anticipated this reaction, but even she was human, and such hostility from people who did not even know her, did disturb her. They even suggested that she was after Rahul's money. Every new tale about her made her more determined to face the music coming her way.

It was a war zone at Rahul's place when he tried to intervene, asking Sonia to stop the character assassination. But the tirade that followed was too much for him to handle alone. The guilt at breaking up his family life by bringing Simran into the picture made Rahul reluctant about pushing Sonia beyond a point.

Rahul had anticipated that his parents would be disappointed but had not expected them to openly support Sonia. His father had stopped talking to him and his mother dealt with the situation with tears, imploring him to reconcile with his wife.

Rahul's mother called up Simran one day, swearing her to secrecy about the call. She discussed the turmoil in their home and wanted to know how Rahul and she intended to resolve the situation.

Mrs Kohli was a strong practical lady; she had enough experience in life to explain all the cons of such a relationship to Simran. She knew he had drifted away and was torn between family duties and his love.

Simran finally asked her, 'Aunty, what do you want me to do?'

'You are intelligent to know what will be good for you. These situations destroy everything around the people who are involved in it,' Mrs Kohli said diplomatically.

As the days passed, the animosity at home intensified. Rahul began to spend more time with Simran now, but it was a different Rahul altogether. The genial, free-spirited man who she adored was missing. Instead, she found herself dealing with a brooding, distant man. Conversations between them were strained and on the nights he chose to stay at her place, there was rarely any display of affection.

As her close coterie got wind of the happenings in her life, Simran knew that it was time to tell Madhu and Ruby about her situation. Simran was nervous to come clean in front of her friends; Madhu's circumstances were daunting and, though Ruby was wrapped up in her little world of joy, she could be far from forgiving. One day, she asked both of them to urgently come over.

'What was the urgency of this meeting, Simran? Why did you ask us to come over immediately,' Madhu asked, concerned.

Ruby and she had rushed over to Simran's place after her phone call.

'Sorry girls, didn't want to alarm you. It has been a while since we caught up with each other. We have never been this slack before,' Simran offered with a smile.

'You mean we have not been able to keep pace with the happenings in your life,' Ruby added, looking at Simran directly.

Madhu looked from Ruby to Simran and back, her face registering her confusion.

'Ruby...I...' Simran started.

'What is going on?' Madhu spoke out, simultaneously.

Ruby relaxed against the cushions of the sofa before saying, 'Madhu, just relax. I am sure Simran has something to tell us.'

Simran looked at her two best friends. She had always shared her innermost and wildest thoughts with them. Why then had she not felt comfortable telling them about Rahul?

'I have to tell you something,' Simran said, admitting to herself that she was uncomfortable.

Madhu was looking at her in anticipation and Ruby just stared at her with a blank expression; only her eyes had narrowed to indicate the intensity of her gaze.

'I have someone in my life,' Simran finally blurted out and even managed a small smile.

'Wow! That's great news. Who is he? Is it someone we know? How long have you known him?' Madhu asked excitedly.

It was Ruby who responded, 'Hold your horses, Madhu. Simran has taken her time to decide that she needs to tell us. Give her time to answer all your questions.'

Simran by now could gauge that Ruby at least knew something. Why then had she not asked her anything? 'Please don't be upset with me, but I needed time to tell you,' she said finally, and added, 'You both know him. It is Rahul Kohli.'

There was pin-drop silence.

Ruby was the first to speak out, 'So it is true! I had been thinking that the news was a product of somebody's overactive imagination. Anil corroborated it... But I still could not believe it, till you called today to say that you had something very important to discuss. I came prepared to pull Rahul's wife away from strangling you to death.'

'Do you really need to be this dramatic, Ruby?' Simran interjected.

'You have not seen drama yet, Simran. The curtains have just risen,' Ruby responded with a cold smile.

'He is still with his wife? How long has this been going on?' Madhu asked, finally coming out of her shock.

'We met each other a couple of times after the Diwali when I first met him at his house. Remember the card party? We lost contact after that and our relationship got serious after a year of our meeting,' Simran revealed.

'Oh my god!' they responded in chorus.

'Are you mad?' Madhu was the first to react. 'Couldn't you see what was happening to me? How could you... Simran?'

'We've been seeing each other much before your problem started. I was embarrassed to tell you guys. I have nothing more to add. I love the man. I am going through a very rough phase and need you both,' Simran implored, tears rolling down her cheeks. She looked at both her friends endearingly waiting for a positive response.

'And what now? Are you both planning to get married?' Madhu asked.

'Of course not!' Simran responded. 'I don't want to get married again.'

Ruby jumped to her feet and Simran flinched at her next words.

'And he will not marry you. Don't be daft Simran. That family is very conservative. Why are you so determined to ruin your life over this? Do you know that you are not the first distraction in his married life? There have been others. He is obviously quite a charmer. How can you be such a fool? Can't you see Madhu suffering?'

By now, Ruby was visibly agitated at Simran and was loud. 'Rahul is not like Raghav at all; he would never leave his family in the lurch.'

'I have to trust Rahul; he has never given me any reason to mistrust him. Please understand I wouldn't do this to myself unless I loved him, I wouldn't hang in there myself. I have never felt this way about anyone ever,'

Simran jumped to Rahul's defence. She didn't want her friends to be antagonistic towards him.

'Having affairs has become a habit with him, and this time also it's going to be no different. Stop being ridiculous and defending him... No marriage...no commitment towards a future... What are you in this relationship for?' Ruby snapped and pointed out various other reasons why this relationship was not healthy in the long run—her family's disapproval, social mockery, insecurity, etc.

'I love Rahul,' was all Simran had to say in response to the arguments.

'You have gone completely crazy,' Ruby went on relentlessly.

Simran had not anticipated Ruby's volatile nature to erupt like this. But her caustic words did more than lacerate her already insecure heart. She asked herself, *had Ruby really assessed Rahul better than her? Had she really become a willing pawn in Rahul and Sonia's unhappy marriage?* All these thoughts made her really uncomfortable.

I need a cold shower, she told herself.

Even as Ruby ranted, Madhu stood up and started pacing the room.

When Ruby stopped, she too stopped in front of Simran.

Madhu said, 'I don't approve at all but will stand by you. I am sure Ruby will do the same. Our friendship is far beyond our personal likes and dislikes.'

Simran hugged her. She needed the support of her friends. In spite of her efforts to always keep a brave face she had been disturbed by the criticisms coming her way for the last few weeks. Now at least she knew that two people were on her side. Two? She wasn't sure about the number as Ruby left without saying another word; she did not even look at her.

Later, on her own, she told herself that she couldn't back away now despite the obvious challenges the relationship posed, as Ruby had so succinctly described. She had no idea what would emerge from the way things stood now.

CHAPTER 16

Simran's family was visiting and she decided to take her mother into confidence.

'You are an adult and independent, but you are being stubborn and foolish and will end up alone and very unhappy,' her mother said emphatically.

When she suggested that Simran leave him and find somebody else who was more suitable, it made Simran very angry. As if she could walk into a shopping mall and take her pick! She felt let down–her mother should have been her pillar of strength. Instead, she had spent her entire trip listing all the things that made this relationship wrong. Rahul was the love of her life; there was no question of giving up now after coming so far. Her mother even wanted to speak to Rahul but Simran discouraged this. When her mother finally left for Chennai, she was a very worried parent.

Meanwhile, all these societal expectations and family pressures started affecting Rahul and Simran's relationship. With Simran being maligned by Sonia's relatives and that of Rahul's, her social outings were a matter of concern.

Rahul did not want her to step out of the house, especially without him. He even started raising objections to what she wore and how she conducted herself in public. He looked at every man with suspicion believing them to be her potential beau; smiling at a stranger also became a cause for misunderstanding.

All he wanted her to do was stay in the house like a prisoner, waiting for him. This was unacceptable for a gregarious person like Simran. Her business suffered and that was something she felt strongly about. She couldn't let her export house be reduced to dust. Rahul's take on the situation was that, that if she stayed out of the social circuit, the negative stories and the gossip would die a natural death. *A completely illogical notion*, Simran thought.

She silently endured as she knew he had disrupted his family life for her; alienating even his parents and kids. The irony was Rahul too never let her forget that he had made a huge sacrifice for her. He often accused her of deliberately killing his peace of mind. His taunts sometimes reached offensive levels. His regular jibes at her, every time she wanted to express herself, further soured things between them.

Their relationship had come under great duress as the gossip mills went on an overdrive; completely destroying Simran's peace of mind, so much so that she began to wake up in cold sweat every night.

'How do you associate with such people?' she often asked Rahul.

To get away from the situation, that threatened to uproot everything that Simran and Rahul had built over the years, he suggested that they get away to Germany for a holiday. Simran did not refuse this time. Valentine's Day was a week away and Simran was longing to have him all to herself. She hoped this would be an opportunity to bring back the old spark in their relationship.

The trip, however, began on a sombre note. When Rahul came over a couple of days before the date of departure he informed her about the huge altercation at home. Sonia had announced that she wanted to accompany him on this business trip.

> 'Is Simran going with you?' Sonia questioned.
>
> 'Yes. But why does it matter to you now?'
>
> 'Now she is your priority. Right?'
>
> 'Sonia, please don't start again. We have nothing in common. And I have work to do. Leave me alone. If you need a break why don't you visit your parents or go off with friends on a holiday?'
>
> He was looking forward to spend Valentine's Day with Simran and there was no way he was going to alter his plans.
>
> 'You bastard! You are so brash to admit that she is actually going with you,' Sonia shouted.
>
> And then there had been the usual abuses, during which he had picked up his car keys and driven out of the house.

Simran and Rahul's holiday this time did not have the same bonhomie like they had in their initial days together. Too much was happening back home! The easy chatter was missing and they would just lie together in silence for hours or walk hand-in-hand without talking to each other. Simran loathed her own life.

Still, it was Valentine season and the spirit was infectious; they woke up cuddled in each other's arms. They had hidden their little gifts for each other and she stepped out of bed, attempting to reach for her present first, but Rahul was more agile and dragged her back tickling her into submission; he wanted to give her his gift first.

They spent a wonderful day together—ate at the finest restaurants, strolled in departmental stores with their mountains of red balloons, soft toys, chocolates—it was so colourful and bright. Every café, every shop was beautifully decorated and lit up. How could Simran and Rahul remain immune to this spirit? Simran loved the various smiling faces around them and amidst the festivities around, they momentarily forgot the past months of stress.

Simran had decided that she would continue her journey to London, and stay a couple of weeks with a friend.

~

Back in Delhi, and away from Simran, Rahul had a lot of time for introspection. He realised that everyone around him was suffering. Rahul asked himself if he wanted to live his entire life with the added burden of having hurt his own family, his children. *What should I do? I love my parents and kids. Should I listen to my heart? Am I being fair to Simran? She is single and has her expectations; she has the right to be happy. But I am married. Sonia on the other hand, for no fault of hers, is feeling betrayed. My parents and children are miserable. Where is all this headed?* He would try to push these thoughts aside, but they would invariably intervene several times during the day, as he went about his everyday life.

CHAPTER 17

As Rahul and Simran tried to rekindle their romance amidst stressed times, Madhu's life was falling apart; she couldn't get through to Raghav and talk the matter out calmly, leave alone discussing the monetary settlement. Madhu was also looking out for front office, administrative, or retail jobs. A very slow, but gradual want, to rise above the situation and build up her life again, seemed to be driving Madhu. She was advised to seek free legal aid; a facility every woman in need, in India, is entitled to. The gratis legal services included providing an advocate in her legal proceedings, obtaining certified copies of orders and other documents during her proceedings, payment of court fee, process fees and all other charges payable or incurred in connection with any legal proceedings. This was a colossal task for someone who had led a very sheltered life. Madhu decided to go for a training programme to understand her fundamental rights more clearly.

The law also had many loopholes; taking up a job would mean no alimony at all or maybe just a pittance. Her pillar to post existence was exhausting. Madhu knew it would be years before she would be able to stand on her feet again. Her desperation often compelled her to send Raghav messages, through friends, for help, but it fell on deaf ears. She had an idea about his income, but didn't know the exact amount he made per month; and he didn't hold back to fudge his papers. He would fake sickness and seek postponement of court dates, hoping he would be able to bulldoze her into accepting what he chose to give.

But Madhu surprised everyone with her resilience and determination to fight for her rights. Her only source of support was her sister and brother-in-law.

Frustrated at his failure to break her morale, Raghav decided to go a step further; he had her landlord evict her from the house. It had been months since he had paid the rent.

At noon one day, Madhu called Simran.

Simran could barely understand what she was saying as she was sobbing, 'Speak up Madhu. What are you saying? I can't understand.'

All Simran could hear was a lot of noise in the background.

'Where are you?' she shouted into the phone.

'On the street outside my house; the court has ordered an eviction and the bailiffs are throwing my furniture off the balcony.'

'What an inhuman bastard! To treat your wife of 18 years in such a way...' Ruby said, after Simran and she reached to Madhu's rescue. They found her sitting on her gas cylinder, on the road.

Madhu moved in with her sister after this.

Meanwhile, an old friend of Simran, Gabriella, who was currently in London, was looking out for a business partner in India. Gabriella, over an informal call to Simran, asked her if she was interested in a business venture together where they would export Indian hand-crafted embellished scarves.

Simran took her time to think about the proposition; her business, although small, was running successfully, *did she really want to expand?* She eventually decided she would, it was just to take her mind off her current predicament in life, she thought she could give it a try. Together with her investments, a modest loan and some monetary help from her parents, she expanded her factory. Gabriella became the buyer, selling to stores in London. Simran got very busy with her factory, tennis on weekends, music classes once a week, and she continued to watch her investments in the stock markets. Simran's dream of having a successful export house was becoming a reality, and she couldn't have been happier. Secretly, she wished Karishma would take over from her when she finished her education. But she also knew as a parent, she couldn't force her daughter to do so and would have to give Karishma the freedom to choose her own career path in life.

Being an entrepreneur, she had to travel a lot; something that did not go down well with Rahul. He often complained that she did not give him enough time. But, this time, Simran was determined to keep herself busy and give some breathing space to this relationship.

CHAPTER 18

Rahul disliked Simran's friends; perhaps he could sense that they disapproved of the relationship. He would often tell her that her friends were a bad influence on her. Simran had anyway distanced herself from the handful of relatives she had in Delhi, who had been quick to judge her and her relationship with Rahul.

One evening, she and Madhu decided to go for a movie. At night, as they were nearing Simran's house, Madhu noticed Rahul outside her gate. It was around one in the morning with just a couple of street lights lighting up the lane. What was he doing at Simran's place at this hour? He came around to the side of the car where Simran was and practically yanked the door open. She realised he was seething with rage. So furious was his expression that Simran thought he would hit her.

Madhu got out of the car; she had been able to sense the fury too. He just glared at her to acknowledge her presence.

'Where have the two of you been philandering?' he hissed in anger.

Stunned by his words, Simran deliberately chose to respond in a matter-of-fact way. He had no business insulting Madhu, *but she would deal with that later,* she told herself.

'We went for a movie.'

'Why for a night show?'

'No particular reason, just decided at the last minute; was tired of sitting at home,' Simran said.

'It's unsafe to drive back so late at night,' he responded, almost hissing out the words as he looked at Madhu, 'Will you be ok driving back alone?'

Simran could however detect the suppressed anger behind this social nicety.

'I'll be fine, don't worry. There is no...' Madhu offered, but Rahul interrupted...

'Are you sure you both went for a movie?'

There was a mocking smile on his face that both women could not ignore. By this time Simran was seething.

Madhu showed him the tickets and as Rahul took the tickets in his hand, Simran glanced at Madhu's face. She had never seen her friend look so angry; the pursed lips and narrow eyes said it all.

Simran had not revealed this side of Rahul's temperament to her friends.

Madhu finally drove away, obviously very upset at the unpleasant end to their fun evening.

'What are you doing here at this time of the night?' Simran asked, trying to keep the annoyance from her voice.

'Sonia has gone missing; she's taken the car without the driver and won't respond to my calls. I thought she may have come to your house, but you were also not reachable. I decided to come over and wait.'

'Why would she come to my house?'

'We had a huge fight. It's unbearable to keep hearing her taunts. She is always in a bad mood and the bickering starts the minute I get home from work. She blames me for the breakdown of our marriage.'

'Rahul, this is becoming monotonous. Find solutions. Don't keep discussing problems,' Simran said irritably.

'There are no easy solutions; I have done what you wanted, what more should I do?'

'Why keep grumbling and telling me all the time what her opinion about me is. I really don't care and I'm fed up.' Simran was losing her patience.

'I can't abandon her, and she can't understand that she and I have reached a dead end,' Rahul was very frustrated.

'Please, this topic is getting on my nerves. Try her number again,' was all Simran could say.

She was tired of hearing him crib about Sonia. The episode with Madhu only added to her irritation. She also realised something–possibly because she had just seen the way he had treated Madhu–Rahul never cared to analyse his own role in their tempestuous circumstances. It was always her fault that she had coerced him to tell his family and Sonia's fault that she could not come to terms with the *other* woman in her husband's life.

'Are you coming upstairs or do you want to go look for her?' Simran asked calmly.

'No, I will come upstairs. What if she comes over?'

For some reason, Simran did not believe him. There was a slim chance that Sonia would head for her home. In all these months, Sonia had never made an attempt to confront her.

She was sure that this evening's episode was just another display of Rahul's suspicious nature. He was unable to get in touch with her earlier, when she was out with Madhu. He had, in all possibility, just come over to check on her and had been caught unawares when she had returned with Madhu and not a male friend. She told herself that if trust had gone down to level zero, between the two of them, then the best thing would be to walk away from such a toxic relationship.

Madhu called first thing in the morning; her voice gave away that she was clearly miffed. 'What's wrong with the guy, Simran? How can he pull your arm, and how dare you allow it?'

'He didn't mean it. He's under tremendous pressure... You know what we are going through,' Simran said, making excuses for him. She grit her teeth even as she said this; Rahul had no right to cause a scene in front of her friend.

'I'm really sorry, Madhu... He was apologetic after you left,' Simran lied, coming to Rahul's defence again.

'Well, he better be, and don't allow him to bully you.'

Simran could sense an attitudinal shift in Madhu. The old Madhu—prior to her marriage breaking up—would not have been so outspoken; the new one that Simran heard over the phone was learning to value herself as a person and speak up for her rights when she saw things going wrong. Simran acknowledged Madhu's resilience, who in turn reminded Simran how she had been putting up with Rahul's illogical behaviour. She felt ashamed of herself.

~

As the months went by, Simran and Rahul's relationship barely scraped through the various forces that attacked them.

Unable to stop people from talking about him and Simran, Rahul turned extremely aggressive, just stopping short of losing control. She realised that the relationship that had brought her so much joy was now the cause of her anguish.

With that also came the acceptance that she was the one who had pushed him to bring things out into the open. *Did she subconsciously hope that Sonia would then proactively end the marriage?* Instead, Rahul's wife had chosen to hang on; making relentless efforts to bring back her husband. Simran saw the way Rahul had passively gone along with the flow of events, unable to make a decision either way. He was desperately trying to balance the two aspects of his life.

Their lives, in the meanwhile, had become a mire of anger, jealousy and frustration, where each was living on short fuse; highly strung and extremely miserable. Sonia wanted Rahul to abandon Simran, which he was not inclined to do. Rahul wanted Simran to lock herself within the confines of her house and not look for a social acceptance to their relationship; something she could not agree to. And Simran in turn wanted Sonia to graciously accept her as part of Rahul's life, and Sonia wouldn't ever accept that fact. So they kept going around in circles.

It became a tiring wait-and-watch game. Sonia was holding on for dear life, Simran was in a rudderless ship and Rahul had a foot each on a boat, with each threatening to topple him over.

Ruby repeatedly reminded Simran of the mess that her life was in. Why was Simran continuing in a relationship that made her so unhappy? Simran argued that Rahul did care for her; after all, hadn't he ruined his family life for her? He thought that Sonia was too dependent on him to even protest. Financially, Sonia might have been strong because of her family background but her conservative upbringing, coupled with the thought about her children's secure future, didn't give her the confidence to just move away, and that too without a fight.

CHAPTER 19

It was amidst this emotional turmoil that Rahul's business began to falter. He had overextended himself and found his auto component manufacturing business buried in debt. His factory had been doing well till he decided to expand and start another factory making brake drums. Simran's astute business sense had predicted that there were slim chances that Rahul would be able to furnish the bank's high rate of interest. His borrowings had gone into crores. She tried reasoning with him that he should expand his business in phases. Rahul had stubbornly stood by the optimistic advice given by a business acquaintance. That person had pushed him to venture into avenues hoping to be at the helm of this new business. The result was that his new factory was state-of-the-art but there was not sufficient business to sustain its functioning. The interest was disproportionate to his income, eating into his cash flow.

Rahul soon found himself in the market, attempting to borrow. Unfortunately, none of the lenders were interested. Paying salaries became a problem and dipping into the company's capital was the only option left to stay afloat. Rahul understood that things could collapse anytime. There was no hope left, except one–Sonia's family. They could bail him out but Simran knew that that would be the last nail on their relationship; the support would be a conditional one.

'I am in a terrible financial mess and had to borrow from Sonia's family,' Rahul told her one day. 'The business was collapsing; I had no choice left.'

His words left Simran stunned.

Didn't he realise that this help would surely come at a price? In a split second, she decided to give him another option. 'Why don't you hand over your business to Sonia and her family? They are very wealthy and can clear out the mess; I will liquidate some of my investments and we can begin from scratch. I also have my export business to support us in need,' she said, hoping to assure him.

Rahul flared up instead.

'What are you suggesting? You want me to give up my sprawling house and live in your small little flat? Darling girl, I am used to huge spaces. Besides, if I move out I will lose everything. You make the most preposterous suggestions! Should I choose to become a pauper overnight? First, you insist I spill the beans at home. Now, this! Honestly, your suggestions are ridiculous. Anyway, I have agreed to take help from them,' he replied.

Rahul's response hit Simran like a physical blow; he was not only openly cheating on Sonia, but was now treating their marriage as a business-bailout plan. She could not hold anything against Sonia's family for surfacing at such an opportune moment to prompt his return to Sonia. They knew how desperate he was!

He noticed the expressions flitting across her face and suddenly said, 'Why don't you give me the money and help me out in my business?'

Simran realised that she might have been an emotional fool, when it concerned personal relationships, but she was an astute business woman, thanks to her years of experience in the stock market. Also, her nascent export business had helped her analyse the volume of money he required. She didn't have the means to stretch herself to accommodate Rahul's financial woes. Even if she did put her entire financial security into jeopardy, it still would not serve the purpose. Besides, she was finding it difficult to trust Rahul's business sensibilities.

'My pittance won't help to repay the monstrous loan that you have taken; let's save it for another rainy day,' she said finally.

'What makes you think that this loan from Sonia's family would have any conditions attached? You just don't have that kind of money to support me; instead you suspect that I'm never going to return your money,' he taunted her.

'It takes common sense to decipher why they are pitching in.' She was ashamed that he could be so brazen about his inadequacy; that he was justifying his willingness to reach out to the parents of his estranged wife when he found himself in a tight spot. Before she knew, she blurted out, 'They want you back with her at any cost. They are rich and can afford to help you.'

'Well in that case, I should be with her, don't you think?'

Simran couldn't believe her ears. It was she who ignored Rahul's malicious herd to stand by his side. But if someone who she loved so dearly, doubted her love over money, then she needed to seriously rethink some of the choices she had made in life.

'Yes, you should. In fact, you should be auctioned off to whoever offers the best price,' she said calmly.

It was then that he suddenly charged at her and then halted. For a moment, he seemed unsure of what he wanted to do. Simran stared at him with cold eyes. Rahul stopped in his tracks and stood rooted to the spot.

After an awkward pause, without uttering another word, Rahul left.

He had belittled their years together by openly suggesting that he would go to the highest bidder. *Did she really want to be with Rahul for life?*

She was disgusted with herself for not realising sooner what she had got herself into. Simran felt the need to go away to some place for solitude and tranquillity. She called her travel agent and asked him to immediately plan her travel to Shirdi.

~

It was an early morning when her train rolled into the Kopergaon station in Maharashtra. She took a taxi to Shirdi. As she got into the car she heard the skies rumble. Simran rolled her window down and looked out into the dreary winding road ahead of her.

She stood in front of the idol with folded hands and prayed for strength. The ambience was divine and she felt an overwhelming sense of peace. She returned to Delhi with the realisation that her relationship with Rahul should end before it gave her more grief.

She turned on her answering machine as she entered her house on her return. There was one voice message from Rahul:

> *Just wanted to find out how you are. Please understand my frustration; I have hit rock bottom and my choices are limited. I do love you and miss you. I just need some time off.*

She went about doing her chores to take her mind off the message. There were too many thoughts on her mind; Rahul, herself, the future of their relationship, Sonia, his bailout agreement with Sonia's family, her future. By the time she went to bed, she was overwhelmed and hid her face in the pillow and cried copious tears. The feeling was like being in a jail cell, being an emotional hostage with no escape route.

Simran woke up the next morning with a headache. Severely stressed, she missed the comfort of putting her head on her mother's lap. Her family had always been her strength, but she wanted to keep her family out of the present state of affairs. Besides, her mother had not been keeping well and Simran felt she could not inflict more pain on the ailing old lady. She would be compelled to come and comfort her.

She was immersed in her thoughts when the doorbell rang. It was Rahul.

Rahul sat on the edge of her bed, held her hand, looked into her eyes and stroked her head. 'My life is shattered; everything is going downhill. At least you should be compassionate. I'm going through a bad patch. It could take six months to bring the situation under control. In the meantime, I have to borrow from my in-laws. I need to think this out practically, leaving emotions aside, and there is no one else who will come to my rescue.'

'But...'

Rahul swiftly cut her off mid-sentence and passionately pinned her against the bed.

'Rahul...no,' she whispered half-heartedly. After going through so much, Simran wasn't sure that their lovemaking would have the same spark and passion. 'Just leave me alone,' Simran shouted and forcefully pushed Rahul away. 'Even now, after reaching such a flashpoint, you crave my body. You are just despicable.'

Simran knew that the spark in their physical intimacy was lost. She acknowledged to herself that things would never be the same again; she would never feel the same way about him again.

When Rahul left that evening, it was after hours of effort to convince her that he desperately needed the financial help from Sonia's parents and that things between him and Simran would not be ruined. Simran only listened; offering no arguments of her own. She heard that speech time and again and she was detached.

~

'I have moved into Raghav's house,' Madhu called early the next morning to say.

Simran knew that the lawyers had been advising her to do so. It was her right under the Domestic Violence Act, but she had been resisting this so far—wondering how two hostile human beings could live under one roof. To fight a bitter divorce and live in the same house with her estranged spouse was a terrible option, but Madhu had taken the step.

'The time had come to put him under pressure. If he wants me out, he will be forced to settle.'

'He just opened the door for you?' Simran knew it couldn't have been that simple.

'I packed a suitcase and went to his house. He opened the door and I just walked in.'

Simran was more amazed than amused.

'Now I will not give him the divorce till he agrees to the alimony amount my lawyers are suggesting,' Madhu added confidently. She added with a laugh, 'When he realised what was happening he started shouting and called the police to complain that I was trespassing.'

Simran was aghast.

'I was really nervous Simran, but it had to be done.'

'I am so proud of you Madhu. Although I still can't believe you actually took this step,' Simran said, her voice reflecting her wonder.

'Do you know what he has done? He has removed all the food from the refrigerator in the kitchen and put it in a small fridge in his bedroom. And he has instructed the cook not to make my food.'

Simran was surprised that Raghav could be so petty. She realised that circumstances could make people go to any lengths to be nasty. But it also reminded her of how Rahul had fallen in her esteem several times in the last year. *Is this what happens when one tires of the other in a relationship? Why does one have to cross all boundaries of decency to humiliate their partner?* But Madhu had stood her ground. She had let it be known to Raghav that she would not put up with ill-treatment when she knew what her rights were.

'What's the news on your alimony?' Simran asked.

'The court has ordered him to give me a miniscule amount of Rs 20,000 a month, which he parts with very reluctantly. I have to ask for it every month and he takes days to give it,' Madhu said, and after a pause added, 'I feel so humiliated.'

'Don't worry Madhu. It will take time, but the courts will sort everything out,' Simran said.

Disconnecting the call, Simran wondered how Madhu had had the courage to do this. *How had her friend, who cowered at the slightest indication of trouble, had the courage to take control of her own life?* And Simran had always prided herself for being a strong emancipated person. Why then did the thought of coming to a decision about Rahul and herself frighten her so much?

~

Ruby tied the knot. It was a small registered marriage just for close friends and family. She looked wonderful in a light pink sari with crystals. Anil looked debonair in his embroidered kurta, especially made for this day. They made an attractive couple.

Madhu and Simran buried their sorrow and participated with full gusto to ensure their friend's wedding was a memorable one.

CHAPTER 20

Simran's share of woes increased. Her mother was taken ill and had to be hospitalised. The doctors suspected cancer.

Even though she was feeling emotionally estranged from Rahul, he was the first person she informed. They drove to the airport together. As she was going in, he gently placed a hand on her shoulder, looked into her eyes, and said, 'Be brave. Everything will be alright soon.' He gave her a hug and she went inside.

She had asked Rahul if he would like to accompany her to Chennai. His unwillingness to be by her side, especially when she was so scared for her mother, once again struck a blow to their already fractured relationship, further souring her feelings towards him, leaving her distraught. She had hoped that, for once, he would put her before everything else. She needed his support, but he did not volunteer to accompany her.

Her mother was released from the hospital after a fortnight. The chemotherapy sessions were to begin soon, so Simran chose to stay back in Chennai for a while to help her settle down. Karishma was happy to have her mother around and Simran felt content and stress-free after a really long time.

Staying away from Delhi also gave Simran an opportunity to introspect. *When did things take a turn for the worse? Was it when I demanded a legitimate place in his life or was it when I refused to bail him out of a financial crunch? Was I right in demanding a dignified place in his life at all?* His willingness to run to Sonia's parents for financial help had been the last straw. She had been taken aback by how blasé he had been about the entire sequence of events.

But wasn't an involvement with a married man the path to a greater cause for misery? Was I really expecting an acceptance in society at-large? The same society that branded me as the other *woman. Am I really willing to live the rest of my life as the* other *woman?* At that very instant, Simran felt violently angry at Raghav and Rahul. She had no words to describe the hatred she felt for Raghav for destroying her friend Madhu's carefully built home of 18 years. Then, how could she ignore everything that Rahul stood for? And how different was she from the woman who had usurped Madhu's position?

The thoughts drove away sleep from her eyes. For several nights, she spent the hours gazing at the ceiling or listening to the swishing sound of the trees or the whistling of the strong winds outside. So many lives were at stake—her's, Rahul's, Sonia's, their children's, parents', extended family and friends—everyone had become a part of this misery... *Was it worth it?*

She called Rahul a couple of times from Chennai to update him on her mother's health; but he had not answered the phone each time; only to call back later. He had never taken the initiative to call or even send her a message. She welcomed his decision to keep distance; it gave her ample time to think things through.

Two months later, her mother's condition deteriorated. It was a difficult time for the family. Rahul, meanwhile, had distanced himself from Simran and her problems. Ruby and Madhu noticed this and pointed out how they had been right about him all along; he would also look at his convenience first before anybody else's. Although Simran was disturbed by these thoughts, she pushed them out of her head. She wanted to give all her time and attention to her mother, whose health was deteriorating rapidly. It was particularly a tough time for Karishma too, who had been living with her grandparents for the last few years.

Simran's mother passed away and this devastated the family. It was Karishma's senior secondary year, so she had to prepare for her board examinations. Hence, Simran decided to shift her back to Delhi later, so she could proceed from there to the UK for her under-graduation. Simran's father, who was frail and not keeping too well, sold off his business units and decided to be associated with the company in the capacity of a consultant. He would spend more time at home with his granddaughter. He would shunt between Delhi and Chennai at will.

Simran returned to Delhi. Rahul's detachment was now more difficult to accept. He did come to see her, but was preoccupied, as usual, with his problems, family and his finances.

CHAPTER 21

Rahul too had been introspecting on his relationship with Simran all the time when she was in Chennai. The things he initially liked about her were no longer attractive to him. The desire and the restlessness to meet her every evening were fading. There were too many things he found troublesome about the relationship now; he wanted to be free of the constant pressure to live up to Simran's expectations. *Why did Simran lead me on to this relationship? She did know I was married, didn't she? Did I ever, through my actions, make her believe that I would marry her? Why then, did she demand a legal position in my life? Wasn't ours a relationship of convenience? Am I entirely to be blamed for the situation that we are in now?*

What Simran did not know was that she was about to receive another terrible news and that too from an unexpected source.

Rahul had accidently left behind an official file at Simran's house and had asked his driver to pick it up.

As Simran and Rahul's driver waited for her servant to fetch the file from the study, Simran innocuously asked how things were at the office.

The driver looked at her sheepishly, and said, '*Memsahib*, please explain to *Sahib* that he is encouraging loose talk in the office and that it will be bad for him. He is already in trouble.'

'What loose talk? You know *Sahib* is going through monetary problems.'

'If *Sahib* is under so much financial difficulty, how can he take his new manager to Mumbai? Everyone in the office is gossiping that *Sahib* has the money for all this, but has no money for salaries. The employees might soon go on a strike.'

Simran felt as if she had been hit by an avalanche. For a minute or two, she was rooted to the spot, gawking.

And then her mind began to race, putting the past weeks into perspective.

Was it really true? Another clandestine affair? No, not possible. I would have noticed the signs. But then, she had been too preoccupied to think of anything else. Is that why Rahul was so evasive about the details of his trip?

Simran was furious. She hadn't even got over her mother's demise and fate had given her another severe blow. Simran gradually started absorbing the implications of this news. She couldn't believe that Rahul was really cheating on her. *Was Rahul just a philanderer who was trying to get away from his mundane life?*

Pushing aside the thoughts running in her mind, and instead of wallowing in self-pity, Simran decided to call him and came straight to the point, 'Is Dipti travelling with you?'

There was silence at the other end. For Simran, this silence confirmed Dipti's presence and she broke out into cold sweat. She had caught him off guard.

'No,' he replied.

'Rahul, please tell me the truth.'

'Cut it out, I have to get into a meeting.'

He obviously didn't want to prolong the conversation.

'I called your office. Dipti is not in the office.'

'Yes, she is on a holiday,' he responded calmly and the line went dead. Rahul had never dismissed her like this before; never brushed her aside like this.

Simran froze, realising where and with whom Dipti was. Instead of shouting and hurling abuses, Simran started laughing. She laughed wildly... more like a mad woman, delirious. It took quite some time before she stopped. By that time, the mad laughter had changed into tears. She screamed, to no one in particular. She had to vent out her anguish. How could she fail to see this side of Rahul? Didn't she know he was a charmer, a Casanova with a way with words, a way with women? Was she this big a fool?

Suddenly, she felt all alone. She desperately needed somebody to lean on. She called Ruby, who came running to Simran.

'You are overreacting. There is no way Rahul can do this after putting his family through so much. He really loves you. How can you believe his driver? He may go back to Sonia, but someone from the office... No way, it doesn't make sense. Don't be silly,' Ruby tried to reason with her.

'His driver was truthful and Rahul was lying. Why is he hiding that Dipti is travelling with him? This time, he has chosen to stay in a hotel, instead of his cousin's place. Isn't it unusual?'

'Now, how do we find out which hotel he is staying at?' Ruby was scandalised.

'I have no clue. He hung up the minute I asked him and his mobile is now switched off. I have to get to the bottom of this,' Simran sounded determined.

Even as they were wondering what should be Simran's next plan of action, they called Madhu over.

'You should have learnt your lesson after what happened to me. We warned you, Simran,' Madhu said emphatically.

'This man has so many problems with his business and now he wants two girlfriends and a wife, all at the same time!' Ruby nodded her head in disbelief.

'Why are you even bothering to find out? Just let him go if you are sure. Don't waste your time,' Ruby said in her usual matter-of-fact manner.

'No, let her get to the bottom of this. She needs to find a closure,' Madhu added firmly. She then asked Simran, 'Are you 100 per cent sure that the office girl is with him?'

'I have a gut instinct about this. Besides, his driver told me, he must have dropped them to the airport. I have to see them with my own eyes to confirm this,' Simran replied.

Rahul's office could not give them any information about where he was staying or when exactly he was expected to return. The last resort was Sonia. The family surely knew when he would be returning. She would have to send the car to fetch him. So Ruby decided to call Sonia pretending to be a business associate who was trying to get in touch with Rahul. They learnt that Rahul would be returning by the 10:30 am flight the next morning.

CHAPTER 22

Simran reached the airport at 10:30 am sharp. She was at the exit gate of the arrival section. The flight had not yet landed and was expected any time soon. Every minute seemed like hours, with time dragging its feet. She felt alone, deserted on an island in the middle of the ocean. Finally, she saw Rahul walk out of the exit gate accompanied by a girl next to him, who was wheeling a trolley.

She instinctively knew that this girl was Dipti.

There was a familiarity between them that Simran could not ignore. They looked like a couple. It was extremely discomforting to see the truth stare at her in the face. Simran did not even bother to look at Dipti; her eyes were fixed on Rahul. This was the man she had loved insanely and who had proclaimed to love her till death set them apart.

Simran gathered her courage and deliberately went and stood in front of them. Rahul's jaw dropped and he turned crimson with shock.

'How was your trip?' she said, looking him straight in the eye.

He didn't reply.

Just then his driver came forward to take the bags. Obviously, Rahul didn't want a scene there. He looked at Dipti and asked her to go with the driver. He then followed Simran to her car.

They didn't speak a word in the car.

'Why did you lie about Dipti going with you to Mumbai? And you actually had the audacity to deny it?'

Simran was ready with her attack as soon as they reached her place.

'There was nothing to mention. We had a presentation and it was necessary for her to come, that's all. What is the big deal?' was his immediate answer.

'You said she was on leave, Rahul. Why did you lie? Since when have you started hiding things about official trips?'

'Stop making a mountain out of a molehill. This is the reason why I didn't tell you. I knew you would misinterpret the whole thing.'

'If it was all so innocent, why was your phone switched off?'

Simran knew all the answers. But she just had to hear it from the horse's mouth.

'I don't know what happened. It stopped working.'

'May I have your phone?' she asked calmly, attempting to squash the fury raging inside her.

When he hesitated, she dug into the pocket of his jacket, where she knew he always carried his phone.

The SIM card was inserted upside down. Simran reinserted the card and the phone started ringing.

It was from the office.

'I will be there in an hour,' Rahul spoke into the receiver and quickly turned the cell phone off.

'I am not blind and dumb, Rahul. You could have been gracious and told me. I would not have insisted that we continue,' Simran's calm façade once again hid the storm raging inside her.

'It's your imagination; I have nothing to do with her,' Rahul said, attempting to take her in his arms.

But Simran pushed him away.

'I think you should leave.'

'Don't be stupid, don't unnecessarily jump to conclusions. You will regret all this,' he resisted.

'You have it all wrong this time, Rahul. I have been losing my health and peace of mind over this relationship, so what I will not take is betrayal,' Simran said firmly.

'You are again jumping the gun, Simran. You know that I love you and no one can take your place. Just think rationally.'

'It's time out, Rahul; you can say what you like but I will believe what my intelligence tells me. I can make 10,000 excuses to convince myself but that won't take away from what I truly think. I don't want to fool myself anymore.'

Rahul just stood there looking at her.

There was absolute silence in the room, except the ticking of the wall clock which indicated the passing minutes.

He then turned and walked out closing the front door behind him.

CHAPTER 23

It was close to a year since Simran had walked out of Rahul's life. Her business was picking up and she had to travel a lot. It left her little time to ruminate over her broken relationship. She kept herself busy, and fit with her tennis matches, music lessons and social commitments. Only occasionally would she think of her past...and of Rahul. *Had she healed well?* Simran thought she did, though she had lost a lot of weight and looked pale.

One evening, as she was reading a book alone in her bedroom, the phone rang. Without moving her eyes from the page that she was on, she just stretched out to her bedside table and received the call.

It was Rahul.

Simran froze when she heard the familiar voice say, 'Hello.'

'How are you?' he asked.

She responded to him with a question of her own, 'How did you think of me after so many months?'

'I was missing you and just wanted to hear your voice.'

She was stunned.

'I want to see you; may I come over?'

Simran did not utter a word.

'I am outside your house. May I come upstairs?' he asked again.

She replied in the affirmative.

Rahul looked dapper, like he was ready to walk the ramp. There was no trace of suffering on his face; instead, he looked fresh and fit. She had been looking gaunt lately, as her friends had repeatedly pointed out. *Was it remorse that got him here? Not likely,* Simran told herself. After all, he hadn't lost weight, his eyes hadn't sunk in, and he did not have dark circles. If at all, he seemed to be as charming and dashing as he was when they had met the first time. *Did he even think about her the last few months?* Simran was sceptical about it.

'What happened? You have lost so much weight?' was his opening question.

'One needs to lose excess baggage in life from time to time. Keeps you healthy,' was her reply.

He laughed; probably not knowing how else to react.

She asked again, 'What made you think of me after so many months?'

'I haven't stopped thinking about you all these months; I just had to sort myself out,' he said, sheepishly.

Simran realised that she could now read him like a book. 'So, are you sorted now?'

She knew she had emerged from this relationship to be more emotionally stable. She had realised that the relationship with Rahul was needed to sort her out as a person. She did not want to judge anyone anymore.

Enough of that! *Things happened...and happened for a reason. She would cherish the good memories and learn from the bad ones. She was an equal party, wasn't she?*

'Rahul, I had invested more than six years of my life running after something I thought would make me feel more secure. But, I know now that I do not need the crutch of a relationship to feel happy and secure.'

'Should we go out for some coffee?' Rahul asked with a smile. Did he think of a fresh start, the same way they had started years back? Was it his way of making it all up to Simran? Or did Simran know better?

Simran smiled and said, 'It was nice knowing you, Rahul... I really mean it... But life moves on, and so should we... I do hope our paths cross again. I will be able to look you in the eye and greet you. Hope you too are able to do the same. Wish you a successful life ahead, Rahul.'

She turned her back to Rahul and faced the window. She leant down on the window ledge with a faraway look in her eye.

ACKNOWLEDGEMENTS

Writing requires courage and persistence. Thank you Prashant, my son, and Mala, my sister, for all your encouragement.

Heartfelt thanks to Ajay Mago, Publisher, Om Books International. I couldn't have met a better publisher who believed in me and my story.

Thank you Shoili Sarkar-Seth, my editor, for patiently getting the book into its present shape.

And the entire team of Om Books International, thank you for your guidance and support.